MarcusT

Renegades of Dome

Also in the Dome Series
By MarcusT

Boundaries of Dome

Destiny of Dome

Anakim of Dome

Other Works by MarcusT

Wyeforde Bridge

Miriam (a play)

MarcusT originally started storytelling to his children when he was a single parent. In those days the tales were not for sharing. Now through the encouragement of friends in the Hastings Writers' Group he completed his first novel.

He lives in the middle of Kent and was by profession a railway engineer. Now in his retirement he has the time and the support to bring his tales to life.

He was the winner of the prestigious Catherine Cookson Cup for short stories in 2012 and has been placed in several writing competitions.

Renegades of Dome

MarcusT

RENEGADES of DOME

The Legend of Kallie

Renegades of Dome

First published 2014 by MarcusT UK

To Cherry, Will, Steph and David, who took the time to read and comment on my ideas, and to Kevin who started it all.

Special thanks to Rosemary and Kate for their support and encouragement.

Renegades of Dome

Introduction

From the heavens, Dome appeared as if it were a crystal jewel, set in a patchwork mosaic of green and golden fields, neat orchards and huge enclosures for corralled livestock. A lattice of irrigation channels was superimposed across the whole area, keeping the entire region a fertile haven in the midst of a semi-barren waste. Beneath its ceramic protection and controlled climate the spires and towers of the city strove upwards while, from their always identical residential buildings, the citizens of Dome continued yet another day.

Generations earlier the Forefathers of the city had a dream. They dreamt of an idyllic life for their descendants, where the pursuit of knowledge and understanding would lead to joy and happiness, and the good of all. A paradise, where toil, sickness and poverty no longer existed, where lives were full and aspirations achieved. A place that would be spared the violence and destruction that spread across the outer world. A haven protected from the final apocalyptic war that eventually destroyed everything but Dome itself.

Each day that broke brought new pleasures for the citizens to pursue, fresh knowledge for them to embrace. Some Domers would gather near the subway stations, others wandered leisurely towards the city centre, either walking or riding the pavement travellators. Few citizens hurried; there was no urgency. All was ordered and orderly as it should be. Mingling with the Domers were the Forefathers' finest achievements: their robots and drones. Vox robots: lifelike yet different; or was it that Domers were like robots yet different? Often it was hard to tell.

Chapter 1
The Girl

There was a certain lightness about her as she walked by that reminded Andy of warm sun, gentle spring breezes and freshly-mown lawns. The Guardian wouldn't have detected it because that level of subtlety was far beyond the robot's cold and unfeeling logical capabilities when assessing humans and analysing their traits. Andy had seen it. It was there when he spotted her skipping lightly up the short flight of steps to the lecture hall's elegant entrance yesterday, and the day had seemed just a little brighter for her presence.

The lecture hall with its high ceiling, gently sloping seating, clinically clean cream décor and cooling air conditioning was typical of all the learning centres throughout the city. Andy knew this, even though he'd never been inside this particular one before.

It facilitated about fifty students and despite not being full was well attended by boisterous, young undergraduate Domers, dressed in a variety of fashionable outfits that were cast in a rainbow of different colours.

The large vidi-screen and well-lit rostrum could easily be seen from every one of the workstations set in front of each light-blue, leatherette, adjustable comfy chair. All lectures at this level of education were delivered by standard Vox robots that appeared to be asexual humans with arms, legs and the expected head, face and torso. The fact they wore no clothes and were covered by dull grey plasticised skin made it clear they were not real people.

Andy was mulling over whether being lectured to by a robot was as beneficial as debating with other Domers, when someone spoke.

'You must be new here.'

Andy looked round, his attention grabbed by the girl he'd seen the day before. She was in her mid-teens he guessed, maybe a little more, five feet tall, slim, with long light auburn hair held by two decorative clips beside her ears, so that it cascaded halfway down her back. Her blue-grey eyes were lightly made up and had a lovely sparkle. She wore a soft pink top with darker trims and matching short skirt. Her blouse hugged her physique nicely without being over-revealing, whilst her tights and soft shoes blended with the upper half of her body. Her cape was across both shoulders in line with current fashion trends.

'Oh, I'm sorry – is it that obvious?' Andy asked, trying not to sound too surprised at her interruption of his thoughts. These immediately changed to being glad she had come over and spoken to him but he hid this well.

'No, it's just that I normally use these two seats at the back and you've taken one of them.' She was almost casual in the way she replied, as if wanting a pair of seats was normal.

Andy was about to query why two seats when she flashed her gleaming white teeth in a sweet smile and continued speaking.

'It's okay; I'll have these two instead.' She lifted her ivory-white cape to reveal its light-blue underside and draped it between the seats to his right. She sat on one of the arms, steadied herself with outstretched legs and got comfortable next to him.

'I can move if you'd prefer it,' said Andy, half rising to do so.

'No point,' she replied, stretching out her hand to pull him back into his seat. 'I'm only here for the first half anyway. These lectures are boring but I need to notch up a few extra Education Credits this term. That's why I take over two consoles. It gets me double Ed-Creds. I want to get enough to ask the Council to change my professional criteria.'

Andy was confused. 'Are you saying you log on twice?' he asked. 'I didn't think the Council would allow that.' He knew at her age and education level amassing Ed-Creds became almost an obsession with undergraduates. It heavily influenced a student's allocated final profession.

The girl smiled. 'They don't, but if you can... Uh oh!' She glanced upwards and broke off her explanations as the lights began to dim.

Confidently she perched herself between her two workstations, leaned forward and began lightly tapping keys on each keyboard to punch in her access and signing-on data. Andy turned to his own console and began doing the same. He stopped when he realised that both her monitors showed acceptance. With one hand on each keypad, she had logged onto both terminals simultaneously.

'That's not possible,' he whispered, surprised at her synchronisation and dexterity.

The girl glared at him defiantly, making it clear that his interest was now not welcome; then she returned her attention to her own screens. Andy, taking heed of the warning, finished logging himself on.

Throughout the first session she eyed him suspiciously between the lecturer's required responses. Her expression made it obvious she didn't like him paying too close attention but he was fascinated at how she could input with both hands operating separate keypads. As the lights rose to mark the end of the first half, she slid into her right-hand seat, still scowling at him.

'You're amazing,' said Andy, with genuine admiration. 'How did you do that?'

'I'm not going to tell you my secrets,' replied the girl, the suspicion in her tone very apparent. 'You could tell the Guardians and get me into trouble with the Council.'

'Then why did you risk letting me see what you could do?' responded Andy, remembering she said she was leaving early and hoping she would stay a while longer.

She shrugged. 'I don't know,' she mumbled, the casual tones of earlier being replaced by a surly distrust.

'That's a remarkable ability you have there, I guess you're pretty proud of it. I bet you'd love to show it off more, but who could you share such a secret with?' Andy smiled reassuringly, hoping to break down the barriers she had erected. 'Look, can't you trust me a little bit?' he suggested encouragingly. 'Honestly, I don't bite and I won't betray you, I promise. I just want to know how you did that.'

At last she relaxed her defensive posture and weakly returned his smile. With the barest movement of her head she nodded approvingly to herself while studying him carefully.

'Give me your hand,' she said, still with a slight suspicion in her tone.

Andy leaned forward, offering his hand. She held it for a moment then squeezed it hard.

'*Ow!*'

She grinned, then let go.

'I don't know whether I can trust anyone,' she said, screwing up one side of her face as if making a big decision. 'You're obviously no robot because you've got soft warm hands; not even the new Super-Voxes could mimic human responses that well. So, I guess you're okay.'

'I'm glad you think so,' smiled Andy. 'I'm just intrigued by what you did. I've never seen anything like it before.'

'Oh that,' she replied nonchalantly. 'I just logged on twice at the same time and because I do, although you said it's not possible, or at least the

Council think it isn't, I get double Education Credits. I want to earn enough to get a trade.'

Andy laughed. 'No one gets a trade these days. They were phased out generations ago when the standard Voxes were built. Drones and robots do all the complex work.'

'Oh, I don't want to do anything complex,' she explained. 'I'd just like to do something a little more practical than debating about things I've learnt. I want a creative trade. It's the only thing I can think of that might help me cope with the weird feelings I get inside.' She shrugged as if disheartened, adding, 'You wouldn't understand, it's just I feel different from other Domers. You're okay because conformity is The Way of Dome and you probably like that; but for me, it doesn't seem to fit.'

'What do you mean, The Way of Dome doesn't fit?' asked Andy, somewhat bemused at her suggestion. 'Everyone in Dome gets an education then a profession and the Council ensures it's the one most suited to their knowledge, understanding and debating skills.'

'Oh yeah,' said the girl defiantly, 'I once caught a glimpse of my life file. It said I have a low probability of making citizen status. So I reckon that means I'll end up losing my mind or going robophobic. I have weird thoughts and hate robots.'

'No way, you're obviously far too bright to suffer a mental collapse,' said Andy. 'And as for fear of Voxes, you should have grown out of it by now; they're just synthetic people, that's all.'

She ignored his comment and carried on, 'I sometimes wish I could get away from them, but robots – they're everywhere. I've heard to escape the Guardians some citizens actually try breaking out of Dome. They're called Renegades. They must be crazy to do that.' She paused for breath and sighed. 'Anyway, the Council says no-one can survive very long outside Dome. If a Renegade did get out, they'd have a short, pitiful life, before catching something called radiation and dying a horrible death like all the people of the outer world did. I just thought a creative trade might help me fit in. I'd hate Correction.' She shuddered visibly at the thought.

'Hey, come on. The Council says that Renegades are just fairy story characters. And we all know Corrective Treatment is only used in very extreme cases,' said Andy, dismissing her fears with a laugh. 'I don't really know what the Council does, but the CT procedure is only there to help the poor souls who can't deal with the education system. From what I've seen you are more than coping.' He smiled encouragingly, trying to lighten her mood. Andy had heard Correction wiped an individual's mind and implanted a new personality that could handle the knowledge it had accumulated. Somehow it made the Domer a different person but he thought he had better not mention this just in case she hadn't been told the same. Either way, just the thought of the process had clearly scared her a lot.

'I can cope with the education and learning,' replied the girl. 'It's not being able to challenge accepted answers that I find hard. We have to conform but I don't always want to. Do you understand what I mean?'

'I can't say I do,' said Andy. 'But I still say no one gets a trade these days and creative skills were rare even when it was possible get them. That's just The Way of Dome. No work and no artistic expertise. As for seeing your own life files; I don't see how you could. They're confidential.'

He could see his negative replies were raising the barrier between them again and changed the subject. 'By the way, I'm called Andy. I'm new around here. Are you local?'

'Yeah, I reside a few blocks away but look, I've really got to go now,' insisted the girl, accepting the change of direction.

'Oh, do you have to?' responded Andy, a little disappointed. 'I was enjoying our chat.'

'Sorry, there's a lecture on pre-Dome literature I want to catch. They're rare, but always worth going to,' she said enthusiastically. 'Then I'm supposed to visit another student to exchange notes on biochemistry. That's boring and so is he; he's kind of juvenile.'

She seemed to think very carefully for a moment or two before saying, 'Hey, why don't you stay till the end and log out all our workstations?' She gave Andy another sweet smile. 'And we could meet up tomorrow if you like.'

'Sure,' said Andy, a little taken aback but none the less pleased at the invitation. 'I'd like to meet you again, if you're sure you want to.'

'I'm sure. I enjoyed our chat. And besides,' she added, catching hold of his hand once more, 'you'd be a welcome change; you're more mature than the crowd I usually have to hang out with. I may end up going robo, but I'll still need someone to talk to till then. You're the only person I've met recently who actually listened when I've had a moan about life. We could meet at the Einstein Diner about seven tomorrow evening if you want?' She squeezed his hand gently, this time adding, 'Please?'

'Okay,' smiled Andy happily.

She let go of his hand, got up, unhitched her cape and headed off. At the end of the row she turned back. 'You will be there, won't you?'

Andy couldn't help but smile again. 'Sure, I'll be there. By the way, what's your name?' he asked quickly before she could turn away again.

'Me? I'm called Kallie; it's short for Kalzamond of Dome.' Then she turned away again and disappeared through the doors.

Chapter 2
The Triad

Ben dived through the thorn bush and tumbled headlong down the bank of the irrigation ditch, taking first gravel, then mud and slurry, with him. A split second later a laser blast ripped through the undergrowth scattering leaves and branches in its path.

He grabbed hold of an exposed root and stopped his muddy slide into the shallow gully several feet below. In spring the ditch would have been twenty feet wide and just as deep. Now, at harvest time, there was barely four feet of water that was no more than six feet across.

Wiping the mud from his face Ben lay on the steep embankment for a few moments, waiting. His heart was pounding like a galloping stallion and his mouth as dry as parchment. The mechanical whine of the armed Guardian came to the edge of the ditch and then stopped.

It had been shortly before midday when the seven-foot, steel and plastic humanoid robot had opened fire. He and Zakoleena had been on their knees digging out beet; his brother had been pulling their cart to the next row. It made Ben's sibling an easy target for the robot's two quick blasts. The first liquefied Enan's head, the second ripped through his chest before he had time to fall. The heat seared a four-inch hole in his torso – destroying some of his internal organs – while the forces within the laser dragged a bloody pulp of intestines from his body and spread them over the ground where he fell.

As he watched his brother's body collapse to the ground Ben screamed at Zak, 'Run!'

They had ducked and dived through the tallest vegetation they could find to keep hidden from their hunter. Brushing aside ripe green maize and trampling golden wheat they had run for their lives.

Once clear of the scene they slowed and made their way towards the perimeter of the farm. Ben knew the Guardian would pursue them relentlessly at a pace they could not outrun; their only hope was to abandon their spoils and get beyond its range. Then a light drizzle had started and finally turned the odds in their favour. The ground underfoot had become softer, which slowed the robot down because of its weight, the moisture partially obscuring its vision system housed inside the transparent dome of its head. It had given them the chance to zigzag to an onion field and the ditch that stood between them and the barren plains stretching beyond the plantation.

Laying there in the mud, Ben wiped the wet from his face again to clear his vision and get his fringe out of his eyes. Trying to control his gasping breath he looked back up the bank. Above him the Guardian had sensed the perimeter of the farm and would go no further. It was still probing the gap Ben had just crashed through, its head rotating first left then right as the sensors inside scanned up and down.

'*Psst!*'

Ben turned his head and saw Zak. She had also taken refuge in the safety of the ditch's gravel. She pointed upwards to the Guardian and made a rolling motion with her hands. Ben grinned and nodded to her as the whirring restarted. He knew he had to move – and quickly. Silently they slid in opposite directions and clawed their way up through the mud, back to the top of the embankment.

'*Yee-ha!*' screamed Ben as he charged at the robot's back. A laser blast hit the bank where he had been only moments before but now he was behind the monster. Zak threw herself to the ground in front of the Guardian and rolled inwards towards its legs. Ben hit it with his full weight. With a random laser blast, the quarter ton of steel and plastic lurched and toppled forward over Zak's arched back. It went end over end then skewed sideways and slid into the ditch. There was a cacophony of hissing bangs and whirring and an array of sparks and flashes for a while, as it kicked awkwardly in the muddy water. Finally, there was a blinding explosion in its head and it lay still as water flooded its control circuits. An eerie silence fell over the afternoon.

Two faces peered nervously over the edge of the bank. Ben put his arm across Zak's shoulders. 'We took him out, Zak. We did it!' He tried to sound enthusiastic.

'Yeah,' she said quietly. 'Don't you think we should go back and look for…'

'No!' Ben cut in quickly. 'It's better you work and I go back for my brother and the cart.' He paused then added, 'Enan deserves a decent burial. I'll only be an hour or so.'

Zak's head dropped. Ben realised she had been hoping his brother had somehow survived and saw in her face the pain she felt. He felt it, too.

Zak stood and slowly walked away. 'Why is it always the Gatherers that get killed?' she asked sadly. 'It's so unfair on us.'

Ben could normally make a joke of anything, but not this time. She was right; a triad of Gatherers had been blasted last week, probably by the same Guardian that had attacked them today. All he could do was catch up with her and put his arm around her again. It was his way of showing they shared the same hurt inside.

'I know how you feel,' he whispered. She let her head rest on his comforting shoulder. He held her closer.

Zakoleena had escaped from Dome two summers ago and had been scavenging on the farm for months before Ben found her: scared, starving and near death.

Since then she had blossomed. Her dark skin showed a deep healthy chestnut brown through the ragged tunic she wore when they went Gathering. She said the short skirt and close-fitting top gave her the freedom to move easily and the material, which was produced in Dome, kept her warmer than her other clothes that were made outside. A tear on one side exposed a fair amount of her left thigh while the missing side panel of her top showed half her bronzed midriff and the curve of her right hip and waist.

Ben liked the way she had plaited her bushy hair, which originally had the appearance of a black seeding dandelion. Now it was in cornrow locks, which hung down the side and back of her head. They narrowed her face and emphasised her large brown eyes and full lips. She had also weaved coloured strands into her braids that flashed different shades of gold, red and silver whenever she moved.

Unlike many Escapers he'd met, Zak was shorter, rounder and curvier than most Domers normally were, and she had broader hips than the boyish-shaped girls of Dome. She jokingly would say she had to escape as they could only correct her mind, not her body. A Guardian had broken her nose six months ago and it hadn't mended properly afterwards, so wasn't quite straight. That was the first one of those robots ever taken out. Nearly losing her that day drove home the realisation Ben wanted her for himself. However, his elder brother had shown an interest and Ben was never able to declare himself a rival. She had agreed to join the two of them in a Gatherers' triad. He felt sure she knew he had feelings for her.

Ben was gone for a couple of hours, during which the weather improved. On his return with the cart he could see Zak had systematically pulled onions from the first twenty yards of each of the almost endless rows of crops she was harvesting.

On the farm each of the neat rectangular fields was huge. The plants and trees were sown in strictly regimented rows that seemed to stretch forever towards the horizon, the rich fertile soil quickly being lost in a blur of green or golden vegetation and the vastness of it all. Dotted around the irrigation channels were menacingly tall and dark pumping stations that saturated everything in dry months. There were also the huge drones that seeded, weeded and harvested. They carried out their functions with a remorseless diligence that nothing could stop. Anyone in their path would be crushed or pulverised as the unfeeling machines went about their tasks. It all seemed so unnatural to him.

Ben smiled to himself when he saw that Zak had piled the onions at the end of each row she had worked. She wasn't the smartest Domer he'd met but she was the hardest working. Between them they loaded her onions on top of the beets they'd pulled earlier, until the low-sided wooden cart with its two large spoked wheels was almost full. They worked in silence. The light was fading and a chill was setting in.

Zak stood in silence for some time staring across the plantation towards the spot where the Guardian had surprised them and, with no warning, blasted Enan. Her face wore an empty sadness; her eyes seemed lost. She helped Ben with the cart's cover then, lifting the yoke to their chests, they set off for home, dragging it behind them.

Less than twenty minutes later they had crossed the bridge the tribe had built to reach the wastelands beyond the farm and relative safety. Still neither of them spoke nor looked at each other. Ben was avoiding the need to voice the painful thoughts that ran through his head.

It was Zak who broke the silence. 'Was it quick?' she asked quietly.

'Yes, it always is,' answered Ben, with equal softness in his voice.

'Messy?'

'No,' Ben lied. 'It must have cauterised at the same time.'

'I thought he was sweet. Oh, we gave each other a hard time occasionally but I was really fond of him.' Her voice sounded pained.

'He knew that; so did I,' replied Ben, his voice gently trying to comfort her.

'I'm fond of you, too,' added Zak, as if to reassure him.

Ben guessed she just needed to talk out the pain she was feeling and the shock they both had suffered.

'I once considered bonding with you both,' confessed Zak, still in a whisper. 'You came as a pair and I didn't want to come between you. The three of us seemed to fit together well. We were a triad and bonding made some sort of sense.' A half-smile flickered across her face.

'Some triads like to bond, especially Gatherers,' said Ben.

As if his voice had got lost in the soft evening breeze, she continued, 'He was strong and you're daring – if not foolhardy. And me? Well, I'm a worker if nothing else. We were a good triad. I felt safe; and now?'

'I'll take care of you, Zak,' Ben reassured her.

'I know you will...' she broke off.

It was a while before she spoke again. 'It was hunting us, wasn't it?'

'It's difficult to say for certain,' answered Ben.

'It must have tracked us for ages, and once it spotted us, it just wouldn't let up. That's why it came out this far.'

'Maybe its programming has been changed,' replied Ben, having to agree with what she had observed.

'But it's basic robotic law – they can't harm people,' she said, sounding puzzled.

'They can't harm Domers,' corrected Ben. 'We're Renegades; the tribe. We raid Dome's farm, and live beyond its control.'

She stopped pulling the cart and looked at him. Her voice was soft and nervous as she said, 'I want us to bond when we get back, Ben.'

'What?' he said in surprise. 'Why? Why do you want to bond now?'

'Because I just *want* to,' she answered.

'Is it because Enan's gone?' Ben asked, turning to her.

She looked fondly into his eyes. With the slightest shake of her head she answered, 'No, it's not like that. It's because everything has changed. The stories said it would happen. We will be hunted down and destroyed. I want to bond before that. You are the only one I'd ever have chosen but I was too scared to belong to anyone. Now, I'm too scared not to. I'm scared, Ben, really scared. I'm scared for you, for me, for all of us.'

He took her in his arms and held her as close as the draw bar of the cart would allow.

She held him tightly and whispered, 'Enan getting killed really hurts. Death has become a reality of tribal life. Bonding is my way of saying life goes on. And, I won't give up.'

Chapter 3
Yan Public

Kallie woke up around nine o'clock. There were three hours to midday and ten until she would meet Andy. The thought of seeing him again made her smile.

Yesterday's lecture on pre-Dome literature had been fascinating. She was disappointed the Council had only managed to save a few documents. There were narratives from the Ancient Eras about Good and Bad, and legends of the Early Forefathers. She was shown things called books – not vidi-books, just books. The Council didn't publish them and said they were too old to be of any real value.

The evening had been manic. She found biochemistry tough going at the best of times. She normally enjoyed note-exchanging sessions as they were usually more of a student level debate than their literal title suggested. Last night, however, she and 'the bore' had been joined by several other student couples and he had assumed they were paired up for the evening. She'd been set up and she hated that.

She'd finally crushed his ardour by grabbing her cape and announcing for all to hear, 'Look, I'd rather swap bodily fluids with a Guardian robot than a creep like you.' She left his residence to peals of laughter, hoping he'd die of embarrassment.

Kallie had slept well and after a quick shower ate a breakfast of cereal, milk and fruit juice, whilst her service unit delivered a pink leotard, blue knee socks, and a green pleated skirt with matching shoulder cape. At ten she set off for another day in Dome. She'd take in a morning lecture, luncheon alone at a student café and then spend the afternoon in a park, considering the notes and work done earlier. It was always the same, always just her.

When she'd reached her sixteenth year Kallie decided to leave her mother's quarters for a student's room. She knew she would then be free to be herself. The regimentation of conventionality would be broken. She would be able to think her own thoughts and do things – her own things. Well, at least in the privacy of her residence. In public she had to conform because it was 'The Way of Dome,' and 'Because it is Good.' These were the Council's stock answers to all enquiries. They didn't seem to understand the question: 'Why?'

After the park, where she spent an hour trying to decide whether to have her contraceptive implant now or wait another year when it would become compulsory, Kallie ambled home to prepare for her date with Andy.

Later, she sat relaxed sipping at a soda in a small café on the far side of Einstein Square, enjoying the final hour of daylight and warmth, and idly watching the world go by.

A few Domers milled around the ornamental fountains opposite, where lights played up through columns of water before it cascaded back down. The floor of the square had a mosaic of a pre-Domer who had wild hair and made some discoveries about space travel. She knew space was the zone above the atmospheric contamination of the planet but, since it couldn't be reached any more, like others she had little interest in the region. The trees and shrubs surrounding the area were a dozen shades of green and contrasted with the pure white marble cladding of the buildings set back from the rectangular retreat. The lecture halls, restaurants and entertainment centres they housed each displayed their wares with neon signs or static illuminated billboards.

She was excited, yet apprehensive, about her date with Andy. He was obviously older than her but not that much. However, there was something about him that she really liked. For a start he was good-looking but – far more importantly – he listened.

She'd deliberately come early so that she could see him turn up and back out if she had a last minute change of mind. She also wanted to arrive after he'd got there so she couldn't be stood up. She'd made a special effort to look nice despite not wanting to encourage him into believing she was a typically promiscuous latter-stage student.

Her tunic was a fashionable pale blue, a little more figure-hugging than the normal standard fit. She didn't think it was too daring, though some older citizens had cast a disapproving eye. She wore her deep-blue status sash left to right, which was proper, then matched it with a silver and grey provocatively short cape that needed another two inches to fully cover the curve of her bottom.

Kallie was proud of her figure, especially her rear, and being slim for her height she was able to wear tunics and capes slightly smaller than her standardised size with the desired attractiveness.

She was musing on how unfashionable oldies were when she noticed a young man not wearing a cape. This was not unusual for young boys, but quite rare at his age. His all-in-one suit was attractively tight yet cut loosely from the hips without being baggy or too revealing. She decided to call him 'Yan Capeless' and not 'Yan Public', the common term for citizens in general. Yan was so lost in his own thoughts that he nearly collided with another pedestrian walking in the opposite direction. It was Andy.

He must have come out of the subway then crossed the forecourt to the square. Had Andy not made a nimble side-step, Yan would have suddenly returned to the present moment, no matter where he was mentally wandering. Andy looked immaculate. His light green all-in-one fitted perfectly, he wore a darker green cape over his right shoulder with the clasp over his heart. He cast a searching glance around the square but obviously didn't see Kallie in the corner of the café and so carried on walking.

Her first instinct was to stand and be seen, but she resisted this and remained seated, watching Andy stride elegantly through the small groups that were gathered in the square. He was one of the few who seemed to have a purpose about them. He climbed the steps to the diner's entrance; at the tall glass doors he stopped and waited, occasionally checking below.

As she watched him, Kallie was glad she had made the effort to look her best. The tingle in her stomach confirmed the feeling; she stood up and crossed the square. Nervously she reached behind and tugged the corners of her cape, trying to regain the missing inches. She'd reached the foot of the steps when Andy spotted her and gave her a warm smile. He was about to come down to meet her when she began to skip lightly up towards him, her face returning his greeting smile. As she reached the top step she stopped and adjusted her cape again. She took a deep breath to calm herself and grinned.

He was an inch or so taller than she recalled. His black hair was swept back and neatly trimmed. They both stepped forward and gripped their right hands on each other's forearms in formal greeting. Kallie lowered her gaze from his hazel eyes to his gleaming smile.

'Greetings Student Kalzamond.'

'Greetings Citizen,' she responded, and released his arm.

'I took the liberty of booking us into the diner this afternoon. I assumed you would like to eat here as you specifically chose it. Is that in order?' His voice was gentle but authoritative, his left arm glided to her back, coaxing her towards the doors.

'That's fine,' she said, allowing him to guide her, 'but can we be, well, a little less formal?' She almost hesitantly added, 'Andy?'

'I'm sorry,' he said. 'Of course we can.' His voice softened, 'I wasn't really sure how to approach this evening. I hoped we could be relaxed, but you know how it's so much easier to go from formal to social than it is to do the reverse. That's why I acted a bit stuffy to start with. I thought you might prefer it that way.'

She smiled to herself, thinking how nice it was to be in someone else's thoughts.

The door swung open on the sensor and a Vox waiter, who had all the limbs and most attributes of a human being but was clearly a mechanical entity, took them to a table overlooking the city. The large amber-tinted window gave a dreamlike appearance to the street lighting and headlamps of auto-cab drones that whisked Domers here, there and everywhere in the gathering darkness.

It was quite a small friendly diner, used mainly during the day by professionals, who would meet there before going on to the debating chambers. In the evening it would be used by different groups for communal gatherings and social get-togethers. Tonight it was about half full. The tables mainly seated four or six citizens and had softly shimmering glow globes at their centres.

Kallie and Andy were led to one of the few tables set for two people. It was discreetly positioned adjacent to an emergency exit. The dim main lighting, soft music, sculptures and exotic plants gave the place a calm and romantic atmosphere. It was far more sophisticated than the cafés Kallie usually went to; she guessed Andy wouldn't have felt comfortable in a food hall that serviced younger citizens.

A Vox waiter came over to Andy and in its semi-metallic voice asked if they were ready to order yet. Andy nodded, drew his credit chip from the pocket of his sash and slid the card into the table slot. His area of the table lit up, displaying the menu. A swift stroke of the position indicator then caused Kallie's area to sparkle into life. She tried to complain about him paying but he swept her protests aside, saying she could pay next time if there was one.

She selected a variety of her favourite dishes to show Andy she had spicier tastes than standard. She also picked an alcoholic wine, her eyes defying him to override her choice. Alcohol was only permitted for full citizens and vocationees but it was common knowledge that the Council relaxed this control in the final year of studentship.

Andy smiled and let her selection be accepted, ordering some bland vegetable dishes and a meat pasta for himself.

'Thank you for ordering, Citizens,' proclaimed the waiter, sounding subservient. 'I can assure you that your excellent selections will be expertly prepared, cooked and brought to you within a short while. In the meantime I, on behalf of the Council, wish you and your companion a very, very pleasant evening with us here at the Einstein Diner. Should you require anything further, please do not hesitate to press the call button on your table.' It bowed and backed away. An instant later the sparkling mosaic table top returned.

'Don't they go on?' Kallie said in a half whisper, as if to not hurt the robot's feelings.

'I know,' laughed Andy, equally quiet. 'I was told that when the Forefathers first built the Vox, they were so proud of the Human Voice Simulator they used the HVS to make them wery wordy wobots.' He wobbled his head like a dotty old debater.

Kallie laughed at the alliteration. 'That's why I like you. I must have known you could make me laugh.'

'Good, I'm glad I can make you giggle.' said Andy. 'You struck me as a happy person. But there's also something sad about you, which is not so easy to understand?'

'Huh!' said Kallie. 'That's good coming from you. You're the one who's the mystery. There's stuff about you that's hard to work out, too.'

'What do you mean by that? I'm just an ordinary citizen, nothing special.'

'Well,' answered Kallie, leaning forward as if to divulge a dark secret, her pretty face bathed in the soft aura of the glow globe, 'for a start, I checked to see if you had logged both my consoles out at the end of the lecture.'

'And did I?' he asked, also leaning forward to meet her gaze.

'You know you did. I got all the credits I expected and more. You must have finished the whole session for me. Thanks.'

'That's okay,' Andy responded with a smile.

'But it doesn't explain why you were there in the first place.'

'True,' said Andy in a hushed voice, jokingly imitating the secrecy in their exchange. 'What made you suspect me of some clandestine objective?'

'You're a full citizen and that was a student lecture. You'd already studied at that level three or four years ago. Hence, you could respond correctly on all three consoles without a problem. So, why were you there? You had better explain yourself, young citizen,' said Kallie holding her nose to sound like the HVS of a Vox, 'or you'll be reported to the Council.'

'Oh no!' he said, sitting upright. 'I am undone!' He raised the back of his hand to his forehead in over-dramatic mock horror.

She dissolved into a fit of giggles, saying, 'You're crazy.' She meant it as a compliment.

'Thanks,' said Andy, taking it as one. 'I suppose I should explain myself...' He broke off as the waiter returned to set the table for them and serve their first course and wine.

A tube at the centre of their table rose to become a cooled cylinder where the Vox waiter placed their wine; the glow globe now gently hovered above it. Around the drink cooler was a warmed rotating section on which the Vox placed half a dozen dishes containing the food they'd ordered, along with other plates of bread and sundries.

Andy poured the drinks whilst Kallie twisted the turntable and selected some diced meat, vegetable cubes and rice for herself. Andy then did the same.

There was a minor disturbance at the door that caught Kallie's eye. 'Hey look, it's Yan,' she said, surprised at seeing him and two companions.

'A friend of yours?' Andy asked.

'No, just someone I saw earlier,' she replied, without looking at him.

The door robot appeared to be wordily explaining to Yan that formal dress was required in the evenings. Yan, now wearing a gaudy cape but no sash, was obviously protesting. He pushed inside and went to a table complaining loudly about robots running everything for the Council. One friend went after him while the other stayed talking to the door robot. Little of the argument was understandable, though Kallie could clearly hear Yan swearing at the Vox.

'He certainly isn't your standard Yan Public, is he?' said Kallie, deciding to ignore them. 'Sorry Andy, you were saying?'

'Ah yes,' said Andy, stirring the food in his bowl, 'I was going to explain why we met at a student lecture hall. It's a bit embarrassing actually.' He paused to pour more wine before continuing, 'My old dwelling was in the South West, Sector 4, where most professional debates are historical. After studentship, I took my two years' vocation on academics to get a science profession. Then a month ago I came of age, was awarded my green sash and became a full citizen. As a vocationee I'd asked the Council for permission to change residence to a more physics-orientated area of Dome. Last week they allocated me a new place to live around here. And, that's why we met.' He paused, ate a little then sipped his wine.

Kallie's face showed no reaction. She was listening and sipping her wine. Her eyes were telling him she saw no embarrassment.

'Okay,' he said. 'This is the embarrassing bit. The reason we met was because, well, I sneaked into the lecture in order to meet you. I'd seen you around during the week and earlier in the day you were checking out lecture times. I thought, wow! she's nice. I went in hoping that you would come back later. I kept trying to think of ways to speak to you without it being too obvious. I didn't want to seem pushy. Then you came right up and spoke to me.'

'You thought 'wow' about me? Goodness, I'm flattered,' Kallie said, putting down her empty glass. 'Why me?' she asked, finding it hard to conceal her pleasure.

'That's easy. There was something about you that said you'd be interesting and fun to hang out with. I'm new round here and need to find a friend or two. I thought that you'd be the best start I could make. You're special. I hope you're not like most students who think a full citizen is off limits. There's not that many years difference between us, and as I guessed you're obviously mature for your age.'

Kallie beamed. 'You think I'm 'wow' and special.' She bit her lip coyly. 'I must admit, when I saw your green sash I was a bit surprised. I didn't think anyone with a profession would want a mere student as a companion. I've still got my two years' vocationship to do. But there was something about you I liked straight away. I felt I could talk to you without being on my guard all the time. And I knew you'd be good for a meal in an upper standard restaurant, at least.'

'Oh really! So I'm just a means of getting company for a meal in this place?' laughed Andy, pretending to be hurt.

'No, of course not, I could come here on my own if I wanted to. I've become a bit of a loner just lately. A place like this is bound to be nicer with someone intelligent as a companion. You're different from the group I usually hang around with. They seem so juvenile. I've had a lot on my mind recently that I couldn't talk with them about.'

'That's right. You were telling me about getting a trade and tapping into your life files or something.'

'Oh, that is just my way of not getting like Yan over there. I'm guessing he finds the education system tough. If he makes professional status I reckon he's afraid he'll spend the rest of his life out of his depth in pointless debates. I sometimes feel like that. The lectures on the Fear Phase of Youth, the time when students blame the Council and robots for all their problems were okay, but you have to take a lot of it on trust. If you're afraid you won't live up to the standard, you know you won't cope with life and that can drive you robophobic.'

She looked at Andy seriously. 'You're a debater of science by profession, okay? What are you actually going to do with the rest of your life?'

Andy looked slightly taken aback, then after a moment or two he said, 'I'm going to improve my understanding and knowledge by debating molecular structures.'

'And after that?' Kallie cut in.

'After that,' replied Andy, 'I want to debate sub-atomic particles.'

'No, I mean after you've debated molecular structures, what will you do with the knowledge?'

'I… I don't understand,' said Andy, looking puzzled by her question. 'I'd just debate to fully understand them.'

'That's because you accept the Council's philosophy, that the gaining of knowledge is an end in itself. I want knowledge, yes, but I'd like to use it too. That's the point of a trade. With an academic vocation followed by a literature trade, I could write a book; a book that can be debated for its own worth. Why do we just debate books the Council publish? I'd love to tell tales of struggling against adversity and winning. I want to publish poems to explore these feelings I get inside my heart. We might all be equal but we're not all the same, Andy; we're not just gatherers of knowledge. Inside we're all different. We're all individuals and somehow that must matter. It matters to me that I'm Kallie. I'm

Kalzamond of Dome and that's important. It has to be.'

Kallie suddenly realised she was pouring her heart out to Andy but wasn't sure how he would respond. She hoped she had found a kindred spirit.

After a moment's silence he said quietly, 'That's not The Way of Dome, is it? You must know pre-history. When the city was first established it was for a distinct purpose. The Forefathers had a way of life that was pure and different from the rest of the human race. Its aim was to bring perfection for them and for us. Why, their descendants even domed the city, to protect it from contamination by the outer world. If they hadn't done so, we'd probably have perished when they did.

'Our Forefathers knew we were to be a higher branch of the human race capable of pure thought and complete learning. We *are* gatherers of knowledge. That's why they arranged for the mundane, routine and basic drudgery of life to be done by drones and computers. When the robots were built, it freed us completely of work and every citizen became truly equal and truly free. The Council's role is to ensure that citizens are provided for and protected. They preserve The Way of Dome. They safeguard our freedom and equality. As things are, you have no need to write a book; the Council has all the books you could want. That's The Way of Dome. To insist on doing something as an individual is, well, almost subversive.' He stopped speaking as the waiter came to clear away the first course but repeated the Council's motto, 'It's The Way of Dome.'

The Vox waiter apologised profusely for interrupting their conversation as it laid out the second course. In another part of the diner, Yan was still creating a minor commotion. Kallie could see this disturbed Andy a little, but she decided not to ask why. She had more important things to find out.

Once the waiter had gone, Kallie continued. 'You're just like all the other Domers,' she said, dismayed.

'Thanks,' smiled Andy.

'That wasn't a compliment; I meant you're always falling back on the Council's mottos. I suspect it's not so much The Way of Dome, more like The Way of the Council. We can be taught and understand but the Council must always be in charge. I once asked a teaching Vox, what happens when someone learns all there is about everything? I was naïve, a child. Its reply was, "Only the Council can know all." I realise now that implies that the Council even controls the knowledge we are allowed to have. Permitting some education and not authorising other information. Think about it, Andy. What is there that the Council doesn't run? Where is anyone's real freedom? Just like that robot, we are all forced do what the Council says we should. Like robots must obey legitimate commands, citizens must follow the Council's will. Don't you see that, Andy? They rule everything and they shouldn't. It can't be natural to make us all be the same.'

'Now hold on,' snapped Andy. 'That *is* subversive. I don't want to hear any more.' His words cut her down as if she were a disobedient child.

Kallie was so stunned by the way he spoke to her she said no more for the entire course. The waiter cleared away without a word this time. It may have been aware of their silence but could have been monitoring Yan's group, who were arguing among themselves. Strangely Andy seemed as concerned with them as he was with her frostiness towards him.

When he did speak he spoke very apologetically. 'I'm sorry. I shouldn't have snapped at you like that.'

'It's okay,' Kallie sighed, the disappointment showing in her tone. 'I just got carried away with my own thoughts. I haven't had anyone to talk to like that before. I guess I just over-relaxed with you. Too much wine I suppose.' She half smiled. 'You're a typically good citizen, and I don't imagine you have thoughts like that. Let's just forget it, eh? No harm done.'

'No harm done,' Andy agreed.

'It doesn't say much for my first impressions of people, does it?' said Kallie, almost to herself. 'I guess there isn't anyone I can really open up to.'

'Come on, Kallie,' said Andy. 'Let's not let one conversation spoil what we might have. I still think you're special.' He reached out and took her hand gently in his own.

She smiled, feeling a little reassured. She still liked him. He was different from other guys. 'Do you mind if I say something now, rather than later?' she asked softly.

'Of course not, go ahead.'

'I want to go back to my residence tonight, and I mean alone. I'm a student but I don't …well…'

Andy laughed. 'I had no intentions of inviting you or myself to any residence.'

'Oh, I thought you would. It's just I've never stayed over with anyone yet. The boys I meet just don't… I mean, I might do one day but…' His straight answer had embarrassed her and she stumbled over her words.

'I know it's common knowledge you students often spend your nights in wild abandon but, as you've obviously begun to understand, as we get older citizens tend to be a bit less frenetic with companions,' said Andy, adding, 'I really hadn't thought of you that way.' He immediately screwed up his face, regretting the way his reply came out.

The disappointment in Kallie's face was obvious.

Then he tried to avoid further embarrassment of his own. 'I'm sorry – that's not exactly what I meant. You're a lovely young woman and very pretty, I'd be crazy not to like the idea but it's a bit soon for me It's only our first date.'

'I know; that's why I said what I did, Andy. I think you're attractive and I didn't want anything else to happen to make you think I wasn't special.' She squeezed his hand and then let go.

They ate in silence for a while but Kallie found it hard not to keep from smiling to herself.

'I was going to ask you how you tapped your life files,' said Andy, opening another conversation.

'Isn't that subversive?'

'Yes, but I don't know if I completely believe you.'

'Well, I didn't really tap them. I just saw them by chance one day back in first standard education. My friend and I discovered if you put an old ali-foil food container over the antenna on the back of a teaching Vox's head, it shuts down and goes crazy, just repeating itself and dancing about.'

Andy grinned at the prank. 'That's because the motor functions are inbuilt but the operational and knowledge functions are sent by microwave transmitters from the Council's massive computer system called Main Controller, MC. You simply put it into a default loop by blocking the transmission.'

'Really?' said Kallie, a little mystified. 'I'm no good at science things. We just knew it was great fun to watch the Vox dance about until the container came off. Anyway, one day when we were doing this, I saw my picture on its console's vidi screen. I don't know why I did it but I hit the show-all key. It had everything about me. It even predicted my future, or lack of it. Under potential profession it said "will not attain". Status was left blank. I didn't understand what it meant but I knew it wasn't good. Now I reckon it's because I hate robots and will probably go robophobic. I guess the Council has already got my profiles set up for Correction when I do flip...'

Andy suddenly interrupted her. 'Kallie,' he whispered with a firm quietness. 'Don't react to what I'm saying but in a few moments two Guardians will come through the door. When they do, I want you to get up naturally as if you're going to the hygiene facilities. While you're passing me put your hand on my shoulder.'

'But...' Kallie replied, not getting more than the one words out before Andy cut in.

'Don't argue, just do as I say, and make it natural,' said Andy, cutting her off. His face belied the urgency in his voice. Mystified, Kallie nodded to him as they watched the events unfold.

Two Guardians entered the diner, one immediately making its way to Yan's table, its movements menacingly deliberate. In size and appearance – having a barrelled torso and clear domed head for its sensory equipment – it would intimidate anyone.

Kallie got up as Andy had wanted.

Yan frantically tried to avoid capture. In a hopeless bid for freedom he made a dash for the doors behind the other Guardian. They remained shut. Kallie saw the desperation in Yan's face turn to fear as he crumbled into a terrified heap at the entrance. The Guardian nearest him turned, moving in to arrest a gibbering, babbling Robo.

The other Guardian turned to Kallie. 'Halt, Student Kalzamond 486.' Its emotionless command froze her hand to Andy's shoulder. 'You and your companion are also required for questioning.'

Alarmed, she looked to Andy not knowing how else to react to the situation. He sat there stone-faced. Then, without the slightest warning, he spun out of his seat and shoved Kallie in the direction of the wall. She screamed at the suddenness with which it loomed towards them and felt Andy's arm lock around her. His free hand hit the emergency escape lever. The portal peeled open as they crashed through the exit and onto a safety chute. A rush of cool air hit her face. They slid for what seemed like an eternity to street level. Andy was on his feet immediately, taking his bearings. Kallie dragged herself up.

'This way,' said Andy, in a hushed voice. He pulled her into a sparsely-lit alley. 'Don't say anything yet,' he whispered. He ducked and weaved through various streets and turnings, dragging her with him.

Kallie could barely keep on her feet so sudden were some of his changes of direction. She saw one Guardian searching for them but luckily a street drone passed, screening them from it.

Andy stopped at the entrance to an unfamiliar square and spoke quietly. 'Sorry if I shook you up a bit but I didn't want to lose you. Now do exactly as I say and don't speak. Their audio sensors can detect breathing at twenty metres.'

A door marked Electric Transport Substation gave way to a sharp thrust of Andy's arm. 'In here...' he whispered. Inside he opened what appeared to be an equipment and tool cupboard and motioned for her to get in. After closing the building's front entrance he squeezed in beside her.

Above the hum of the electrical machinery she heard mechanical footsteps approach, and then the lock turned. Through the ventilation slats of their locker she saw the room flood with light. In fear, Kallie stopped breathing. The hum rose and the whole room trembled to the familiar sound of a subway train passing beneath them. As the noise died the Guardian left and darkness engulfed the room once more. Kallie released her breath.

Andy touched her mouth for silence. 'Okay it's gone,' he said, half falling out of the cupboard.

Kallie was too scared to move until he gently helped her out. She nervously looked around the room recognising nothing.

'What's going on?' she whispered, barely raising her voice above the hum.

'We were lucky with the train,' answered Andy. He slid his arms around her neck reassuringly 'Kallie, will you trust me totally?'

She nodded and joked nervously, 'Do I get a choice?'

Andy smiled, 'Good. In a while I'll take you to my residence. Once inside you're safe. Just don't answer the door or use the terminal. Do you understand?'

She nodded and gave him an ironic grin.

'I'll be back with you as soon as possible, and then I'll explain everything I can. I think we've just got us a whole bunch of problems to sort out but we won't let that spoil our date, eh?'

A little while later she closed the door of his residence behind her and leaned back on it. She linked her fingers, and with her hands holding the back of her head breathed out fully for the first time in what must have been ages. At last, after more than an hour, she felt safe. Before he'd left Andy had said she'd be safe here and somehow she knew she could believe him.

Chapter 4
The Council

Six doors slid slowly open. Stepping forward with unified regimentation, the six Councillors took their places, two by two, at the three benches angled against each other that were clearly their traditional positions. Each wore an elegantly-cut tunic, matching cape and a golden sash of office. Their faces were etched with years of experience and knowledge. Their postures displayed all the bearings of serene power and benevolence. The seventh place was a curved arc opposite and between the first and sixth Councillors' locations. The arc above the half hexagon made by the desks with the six-pointed star of the Council at its centre was traditionally the emblem of Dome. The counters were inlaid with vidi-screens, workstations and keypads. The large double doors into the circular chamber that led to the seventh place and the counter from which the Domers could address the Council remained shut.

The chamber itself was large with a domed ceiling, which provided light that cast no shadows. The walls were cream with light tan marking for the doors and the flooring was soft green. There were no windows as the chamber was housed in one of the many levels below the city of Dome. The air conditioning silently kept the atmosphere perfect for

Domers. Domers were not expected to attend the meeting, because none had addressed the Council for generations. The Councillors remained standing.

Councillor Arten, with his long face and pointed chin, which had not a hint of hair, pulled himself to his full height. His small, piercing eyes regarded each of his companions with slight mistrust as he began the proceedings by saying, 'I have called you fellow Councillors here because, in my capacity as Law and Order Governor, I have reason to believe that the city faces a major threat to The Way of Dome.' His spindly fingers stroked a few keys of his pad and the monitors before each of the other Councillors displayed an analysis of the situation.

'I don't see any reason for not communicating in the usual manner,' said one of the Councillors.

'That is because, Councillor Tusie, you do not handle hard facts very well,' Arten told his female critic curtly. 'If you did, many things would become quite apparent to even an Arts and Leisure Governor. Information from Councillor Forrell indicates that, from beyond the perimeter of the plantation, something or someone continues to threaten food supplies – to such an extent, I might add, that the farming drones are unable to eliminate the problem with the normal pest control arrangements.' Arten leant forward on his thin arms, placing his hands either side of his keypad, while the others digested his comments.

'That is correct,' confirmed Councillor Forrell, who was stockier than Arten but equal in height. His round face, full head of long hair and beard gave him the appearance of a sage, one endowed with years of wisdom. 'Councillor Arten controlled the problem for a while with additional Guardian patrols but just recently the foragers have increased their activities again.'

Tusie directed her objections to the assembly in general. 'I still don't see why we could not deal with this problem without coming to the Chamber.' As she spoke she jerked her slightly tipped head side to side vigorously, causing her shoulder-length hair to swish and her fringe to twitch across her forehead. Her slanting eyes, button nose and small thin mouth were demanding an answer.

Arten obliged. 'Because my dear Councillor,' he said, 'after my proposed action is agreed, one of us will have to make a vidi-cast to the city. Also, we do not have the authority to act further than I have done already without higher levels of approval. Indeed, the reprogramming I initiated pushed legalities to the limit.'

'Could we not optimise and act independently of the higher monitoring?' suggested another Councillor, who had close-cropped hair and ebony skin tones, adding, 'We have before.'

'That is one of my alternatives,' replied Arten, knowing he needed at least seventy per cent compliance to support his action. 'Let me explain. When, despite using city Guardian patrols, raids increased again, I actioned several armed Guardians, with little success. However, the loss of city Guardians allowed an increase in subversive activities, so they were recalled. Most subversives, I am glad to say, are now in custody and awaiting treatment. Further action was still required to prevent the subversives who have escaped and become Renegades from taking our food. I deduced Renegades were raiding the farm as, by robotic law, Guardians cannot actually harm humans and my patrols had had no further success. Finally, I reprogrammed three armed Guardians to identify any living forager on the farm as vermin and a threat to the citizens of Dome. Raids immediately ceased. Success, I assumed, but no – after a while they restarted. In the last six months two of my armed Guardians have been immobilised. Therefore, to protect the city's food supply, Councillor Forrell and I agree we must arm a squad of city Guardians and extend their range in order to destroy all vermin on or near the farm. I have calculated there would be an upsurge of subversion in the city during this action but a vidi-cast warning should minimise this until the Guardians return. All I need is the authority or an optimised decision. Which is it to be?'

'You want us to optimise a robotic war against vermin, who are, by your own deductions, humans and ex-Domers?' The cry was as emotive as Tusie could manage.

'No, Councillor Tusie,' Arten replied coldly, 'I want another alternative, but I see none. Do you know of one? If not, then we have three choices. Get authority from MC, which we could not. Optimise my proposals, which we can. Or watch The Way of Dome die, which we cannot allow.

Remember, if the subversives inside the city ever become allies of those vermin outside, our problems will be a thousand-fold greater.' He refrained from adding that two dangerous subversives had evaded arrest that very evening.

The meeting closed with five votes to one. Councillor Tusie required more time to process her thoughts. Councillor Arten had his seventy per cent so disregarded her as a rogue point. There were no control factors and a past precedent.

Chapter 5
Crazyman

To Zak's surprise her union with Ben had been much anticipated by the women of the tribe, who were delighted to put on a celebration banquet. She was presented with a beautiful white bonding cape by one of the girls who had married earlier that year. The cape had been made from the soft layer of a split hide which had been a hunter's trophy. It was then soaked in urine for a month to remove the colour, scraped to improve its softness and washed thoroughly to eradicate the effects and smell of the process. Zak would pass it on to the next bride of the clan.

The festivities took place in a derelict football stadium and began at sun up, when many of the families around Ben and Zak's shelter came by with breads, fruit, meat and vegetables. By mid-morning there were fifty or sixty different groups preparing food and drink for the feast, and chatting happily. At mid-day the elders of the tribe arrived along with the musicians and the rest of the folk who weren't out gathering or hunting. Zak guessed there were perhaps three or four hundred people who had come especially for her and she couldn't help but wear a beaming smile every time someone wished her and Ben well and many children.

The ceremony was conducted by one of the elders, who celebrated how the tribe had resurrected bonding in defiance of Dome's practice of controlled single child and single parenting to maintain exact numbers. The whole gathering sang a couple of songs. One was celebrating the tribe's need for numerous children, the other wishing long life and happiness to the couple. Then Ben and Zak promised to be true to each other in front of the whole tribe. The tribe responded with three rousing cheers, led by the elders. Tela, the senior elder, took a knife and carefully cut Zak's shoulder and removed the silver contraceptive capsule the Council had fitted in her arm before she had escaped. Crushing it beneath his foot he pronounced them a bonded woman and bonded man of the Renegade tribe.

Things went quiet for an hour whilst everyone went home to change into their most colourful and flamboyant clothing. Then the partying began. From mid-afternoon until well after dark the tribe danced, sang, ate and drank in happy celebration. Children ran around playing games and grabbing food as they chased each other through the crowds. Life was normally very hard, but a bonding feast was a chance to forget and be joyful.

Eventually everyone drifted off back to their shelters and she and Ben went home exhausted, but content.

Zak lay still, listening to the night sounds that crept through the ruins of the small town that was the home of the Renegade tribe and far beyond Dome. Most of the buildings had been destroyed in the war that annihilated the outer world and were either burned down or piles of rubble from what she was told were called bombs or missiles. Their shelter, like those of many of their fellow Gatherers, was in the derelict stadium. It had places to live under the seating stands, and the large communal open area at the centre was where the bonding feast took place. Also people could meet and congregate there.

The outer walls of the arena on one side and the terraces on the other provided the occupants with protection from the weather. The passageway that ran most of the way round the complex allowed ease of movement regardless of the conditions or need to go outside.

Ben's body felt warm cuddled against her back as he slept. She was nervous of moving in case she woke him. She felt safe in his strong arms and in the warm glow of the fire by the entrance of their shelter, but she couldn't sleep. Not that she wasn't tired, she was.

Physically she needed to sleep but her mind kept her awake, which was unusual. Much was changing, not just for her and Ben but for the whole tribe. Was it really like Crazyman foretold – the beginning of the end?

She had never met Crazyman, he had died a few years before she escaped, but stories of him were told over and over again. She tried to trace his face in the shadows and shapes of their shelter but couldn't do justice to his weasel-like features, crazy grin and staring eyes. Shadows could never be the squeaky voice that everyone said he had.

Zak had been told Crazyman was a Seer who just appeared one day fifteen years ago, when Ben was a child and before the tribe began. He was the one who brought them to the ruins. Before him, Renegades lived and died on the plantation. Many starved to death since the food they found needed processing to be edible, and they'd never learnt to prepare anything they ate inside Dome. Others suffered fatal accidents or poisoning. A few, being too weak with hunger to get out of the way of the huge farm machines, were killed as the drones worked their way relentlessly across the vast fields. If they survived the rigours of their environment, other Renegades often stole what little they had. Ex-Domers were accustomed to being given, or taking, what they needed. The Council and robots had always provided for them.

Crazyman had found the ruins outside the farm beyond the reach of the machines and he also found a way of banding the dozens of competing Renegades into the beginning of the tribe. Fruit and a bell were his tactics. He sat in the middle of the town square with a large pile of fruit he had spent the week collecting. Every so often he would leave his feast to ring the bell in the old tower. Curiosity and hunger did the rest. No Renegade could afford to pass up a free meal.

As they ate Crazyman scampered here and there saying, if they worked together, they would all have enough to eat. The competing Renegades quickly realised he was right and that they were safer in the ruins and so stayed. That began the Gatherers; these were Renegade raiders who slipped in and out of the farm to get food, and they did live much better.

Once he had taught the Renegades how, what and where to gather, Crazyman didn't do it anymore. He spent his time darting around the ruins; he was always searching, peering into dark corners and down darker, deeper holes. He found all manner of things; some were useful, yet with other finds he only had vague ideas of what they were for but that didn't deter him. He must have been a strange sight with his straggly hair and goatee beard. His clothes were too small to fit, and his body was so thin that he always looked in need of a meal. But he had two great qualities that won him respect and kept him fed. Firstly, he was a great storyteller, constantly grinning as he entertained the tribe with his stories. Secondly, he was invariably right when he said he was.

The legend says one night some of the tribe were sitting around a communal fire telling stories when he brought over a metal pot he'd found. It was full of water. Crazyman dumped it on top of the flames and just sat there watching it, grinning. When it started to bubble he scurried off. He came back with some inedible tubers and tossed them in the boiling water. He danced about excitedly saying, 'That's how the Council processes food: with fire and water.'

Crazyman rediscovered cooked meat in the same experimental way. After burning the feathers off a dead hen, he found it edible. 'We should catch and eat the animals,' he said excitedly. 'That's why they are kept on the farm. It's what they are for.'

The first three Gatherers volunteered to hunt for food. Though not easy it was little more than chasing and catching chicken, sheep, pigs, or cattle in their corrals. They learned to fish, too. They were then a tribe of hunter gatherers.

Crazyman had tales, many tales. Before he escaped from Dome he was a historical professional. He claimed all his knowledge and tales came from the old Dome and pre-Dome periods. To use what he knew was only a matter of sorting the truth from the Council lies, and experimenting instead of debating.

Sometimes he would lose his grin and talk about the future. He would shake his head and say, 'The Council won't let us stay Renegades. If they find our tribe, they will have to destroy us. They can't live in peace, they have to dominate and destroy everything they can't control.'

He had tales of the outer world too. He would say, 'It was like an angry beast, it could not even rule itself. There were countries and factions who were constantly at war. Eventually that led to self-destruction. It even tried to destroy Dome but was beaten back by the Forefathers.'

Crazyman claimed he could see their destiny. It was to free Dome from Council control but, unless they found the way and the twin towers, they were in danger of being hunted down and destroyed by the Council.

Zak woke with a start. Ben was already up and tending the fire. 'Sorry about the smoke,' he said, trying to stop it wafting into their shelter. In his sooty sweatshirt, shorts and jacket he looked as if he had finished second in a wrestling match between him and the billowing effects of his blaze. 'The wind has changed since sun up. Are you okay?'

Zak sat up hugging the blankets around her and joked, 'I can't answer difficult questions like that first thing.'

Ben brought her a warm fruit drink. 'We rest today,' he said. 'It's our honeymoon. We'll take a walk to the lake, maybe watch the fishers at work and perhaps have a swim.'

'That sounds nice,' mumbled Zak. 'I can tell you about my strange dream. I dreamt that Crazyman was talking to me. Telling me tales, but I can remember it all so clearly.'

She sat there a while and admired Ben, her husband, still wrestling the smoke. She was a complete woman now that she was bonded to him. She knew Ben would remain Ben, always a boy at heart. Having been born outside Dome he hadn't even had standard education. He made up for that with wit and daring, and had no hang-ups left over from Council indoctrination. The hard tribal life had given him a strong, handsome, bronzed body. She would have to do something about his unkempt, blond shoulder-length hair and what she called his "nearly beard". But she wouldn't change him, not her Ben.

Chapter 6
Vidi-cast

Kallie woke reluctantly at the touch on her shoulder. She turned in an unfamiliar bed to see a vaguely familiar face.

Andy stood above her, coffee in hand. 'Here, try this,' he said.

She blinked, reached out and took it gratefully. 'What time is it?' she asked, still bleary eyed.

'Six after ten.'

'Oh!' she said, after taking a sip, 'I'm not at my best at six after anything, am I?'

'You're fine and after breakfast I'm sure you'll feel even better,' said Andy. 'I've ordered it for ten-thirty. Is that okay?'

'What…?' Kallie sat up. '…take it a bit steady, will you? I'm a girl. I need time in the morning just to remember what I have to do, like shower, dress, makeup; breakfast comes way down my list.'

'Okay, okay, I get it. I'll put breakfast on hold and we can eat when you're ready. Use the service unit for anything you need, it's a standard catalogue.'

Kallie ran her fingers through her tangled hair, kicked her legs out of the bed and sat up.

'Yuk! I slept fully dressed. What a mess.' She shrugged off the bedcovers, stood, slid out of her clothes and went naked to the service unit, punched in a towel order then headed to the shower in the corner. It was the same as any other standard Dome bathroom except Andy's was a gentle grey; she'd had hers done crimson.

The Council permitted Andy, as a full citizen, twice the space in his residence compared to what she was allowed. It was still a single room with a bed, shower, screened toilet, and service unit. However, although he had a desk and study area as she did, he also had a separate dining area and a relaxation corner with comfortable seats, loungers and a small central table for vidi-books and board games if he wanted them. Her work-centre doubled as both of these. Typically, he'd had his residence decorated in distinct colours marking out the walls and floor of each area.

'What happened last night, apart from you not finding me that attractive?' she asked sarcastically whilst enjoying the piping hot spray. 'How did you know those Guardians were coming?'

'I guessed,' answered Andy. '… and I wouldn't be so sure of me not finding you attractive today. You look pretty good first thing in the morning from where I'm standing.'

'What? Hey, don't be so cheeky!' Kallie pulled the screen across her nakedness in embarrassment at Andy's reply. 'Wait a minute – you can't guess a Guardian is coming.'

'You can if you see them through the window,' he laughed. 'It was obvious that Yan was going robo, so they were bound to show up. That's why I tried to stop you sounding like a subversive in public. The waiters would have been monitoring all conversations in the restaurant, including ours. It's not unusual these days.'

'Thanks for getting me out of there. I owe you one,' said Kallie, hitting the warm air button to dry her skin. Wrapped in a huge fluffy towel delivered by the service unit, she punched in the codes for some new clothes and came back into the living area.

Ten minutes later the dispenser produced a purple and gold top, pink skirt, and a mauve cape with black trims. She disposed of her old clothes and the towel via the recycle chute and called up breakfast when she was dressed.

Whilst eating a stark realisation hit her, killing her appetite. She pushed her cereal bowl away at the thought. 'Andy, that Guardian knew my name.' She couldn't hide the sudden panic in her eyes. 'I'm known to the Council,' she said desperately.

'Kallie you've been running risks for ages. It was bound to happen,' said Andy.

'But it was only Ed-Creds. That's not subversive,' she pleaded, looking for reassurance, but finding none.

'Kallie, you were literally stealing them. That's anti-standard behaviour and you were beating the system. The Council can't allow that, it's not The Way of Dome.'

'But, but...' She was lost for words and fell silent.

'I'll help you,' said Andy quietly. 'If I can work out a solution, I'll do what I can to get us out of this situation. But I must admit it doesn't look good.'

She looked up at him again. 'Why? Why would you help me, when we've only just met?'

Andy shrugged, 'Because, you're you. You're special, remember? Besides, I was with you. They will know me through association. But they probably know me in my own right, too.'

'Will I be arrested?'

'We both will.'

'Both?' said Kallie, surprised.

'In all probability; But with luck they won't find us here for a while, which gives us time.' He reached across and stroked her cheek as if to reassure her.

She gripped his finger and half smiled. 'You'll stay with me until I'm arrested, won't you?' she asked in a whisper.

'What? You mean you give up, just like that?' The disappointment in Andy's voice showed.

'What else is there but correction or detention? I just wanted to know if you'll be with me to the end.'

'I promise you, whatever happens; I'll be there with you Kallie, to the end.'

'Thanks,' she smiled and fully took hold of his hand, squeezing it gently. She recalled how only a couple of days ago his warm hand had started a chain of events that now locked their destinies together in more ways than one.

'I'm sorry,' she said softly. 'But for me you wouldn't be, well…'

'I would,' said Andy. 'You have all the feelings and ideals I have, only I've learned to keep them hidden from everyone, including myself and the Council. As a science professional I was trained to deal with facts in a logical, almost detached, way. I was cold. But it was getting harder and harder not to let my feelings show. You showed yourself because you're openly beautiful. That was the something special I talked about last night. I'm trained to be logical – but you? You have inspiration. You're a beautiful and creative version of the person I feel I am inside.'

Kallie smiled and screwed up her nose impishly. 'Well, if we have a few days left, I'm going to enjoy them.' She bit his finger playfully.

'*Ouch!*' he laughed.

Their conversation was interrupted by the vidi-screen, which suddenly glowed and then burst into life. The Council had always had the ability to interrupt the citizens' lives with vidi-casts into their homes and to the street screens when an important announcement or citizens' advice broadcast was to be made. The announcement was preceded by music and views of idyllic city life, during which Andy cleared the table to the waste chute. In Dome everything was sent to be recycled. The music and views faded and a thin benevolent face appeared.

'Greetings citizens, may you be content in your pursuits. I am Councillor Arten, your Law and Order Governor. It is my privilege to serve you and my duty to bring you this news. From today you will notice there is a reduced force of Guardians on duty. There is no need to be alarmed about this, because you will still be fully protected by those Guardians who remain.

'The reason for this reduction within Dome is that the Council and I are constantly monitoring situations in the outer world beyond our city, as well as events inside our home. Our analysis of everything we have observed: the events, trends and the environment, indicate we need to deploy a task force of Guardians on a specific project to ensure The Way of Dome continues uninterrupted.

'To balance this necessary action, we ask that you, the citizens of Dome, are most diligent in reporting any disruptive activities you become aware of.

'Any subversives should heed our warning. Nothing will be allowed to disrupt The Way of Dome. Persist in your activities and you will be dealt with most firmly.

'Citizens, remember The Way of Dome is good. Those who cannot conform will be helped with corrective and normalising treatment. Your duty is to help them by bringing them to our attention. Your Council cares.

'May The Way of Dome be with you; always.'

Arten's face dissolved into a blank screen.

'That's strange, an override vidi-cast for internal security,' said Kallie.

'It's significant,' said Andy, sounding puzzled. 'Not only that, most citizens would still be at their residences right now with their vidi-screens on at this time of day. It's unlikely anyone would have missed it.' He set to re-run the vidi-cast. 'See, if you were watching anyway it blends into a normal viewing as the final item of a news cast.'

'Okay, so what does it signify that we don't already know?' asked Kallie.

'I'm not certain,' replied Andy, still sounding puzzled.

'Well, I'm known to the Council, and so will you be no doubt,' said Kallie, listing her thoughts. 'There are now fewer Guardians, but obviously they will be operating at higher detection levels. We're both likely to be arrested if we leave here. Eventually we will be traced and detained. Then there's Corrective Treatment, where we are turned into good citizens with a new life elsewhere in the city. But, as long as we are together, I'm going to be as happy as I can. After Correction I won't know anything about this nonconformist life I'm leading, so I've got to live for now.'

'It was an override,' said Andy, still sounding concerned. 'That only happens when every citizen must be informed of Council actions because the citizens of Dome may wish to override or ratify their decision. The citizens never contradict the Council's verdicts but it is in the Constitution of Dome. Or it could be for safety reasons when Dome itself is in danger. It's like the time when outer world storms threatened to damage Dome.'

'Oh yeah, I remember that. I was only small at the time,' said Kallie.

'I bet you're not much bigger now,' joked Andy

'Hey, don't be hurtful. I thought you said I was attractive?'

'So, you're small and attractive. I like that,' quipped Andy. He replayed the vidi-cast again.

Kallie ordered some make-up from the service unit and, while Andy ran over the message several times, she did her face and nails sitting behind him on the bed.

'There's something big happening,' said Andy, 'I'm trying to work out what it is. There must be a major threat to Dome, otherwise why would he say necessary action?'

'Do you think it's us?' asked Kallie, holding her hands out to dry.

'I doubt it. I hear nonconformist activity has increased lately but that should mean increased patrols, not a reduction. It doesn't seem logical.'

'It is if they mean smaller normal patrols while those Guardians taken out are upgraded,' said Kallie. 'They could then purge the city in just a few days. Every subversive detained in one fell swoop.' She stood up. 'How do I look?' she asked.

'Considering the problems we have, you look lovely,' replied Andy, after taking a long glance over his shoulder. 'But your cape's a bit short, isn't it?'

'Not if you're the only one seeing me,' she laughed. 'I'm trying to ignore the problems and stop you fretting.'

'You could be right about the purge, you know. It makes some sort of sense, I have to admit that,' said Andy.

Kallie slipped her arms around his neck and held her face close to his. 'Besides, is there any point in me being shy? If you're right, we only have a few days together, a week at the most. I'm with you now and you're all I'll ever have before they correct me. Afterwards I probably won't remember anything so I won't even feel guilty or have any regret, whatever we do.'

'We're not done yet. There are a lot of things we could do to show the Council we have normalised. We don't have to give up immediately.'

'You may be okay, but as you said, I've been stealing Ed-Creds for ages. The Council is uncompromising with anti-standard behaviour.' She pulled herself closer, snuggling into him. 'I don't have many long-term options, do I? Let's face it: eventually it will be Correction, or Correction. So, I've got to make the best of my last few days as me.'

Andy reached up and held her arm across his chest. 'We could try and escape,' he whispered.

'What?' She broke free. 'Are you mad? We could never get out of the city and even if we did, we would starve to death on the farm or die of some terrible disease like radiation, or get crushed by a farm drone. I've heard they're gigantic.'

'Do you want Correction? Do you want to lose what it is that makes you special? What makes you Kalzamond of Dome? Kallie, I'm sure we could survive outside. I want us to. I know together we could do it.'

'Andy, outside is the only thing I know of that's worse than Correction. It's certain death. The Council says–'

'The Council's probably lying,' Andy assured her.

'That's subversive. They have to tell the truth, it's the law,' retorted Kallie. 'They cannot lie.'

'They cannot lie about Dome; but they can bend the truth,' replied Andy. 'You said as much last night. And the Council can say what it likes about the outer world. Dome laws only apply to the Council inside Dome. Yes, Renegades are likely to die out there but some, just a few, must survive. My logic tells me that must be true. If some can survive, then together *we* can. We could, I know it. We're near the rim here and there are ways out, otherwise there would never be any Renegades.'

As he spoke he stood up and took her in his arms. 'Kallie, we have no future here, not together. We have to escape Correction, it's not for us. I will gladly die for you, or strive to be free with you. From the moment I saw you, I knew it. Without you my whole existence amounts to nothing more than a professorship in pointless debates and, like you said, we're more than that. We must be.'

'But Andy, we…'

He pressed his finger on her lips gently. 'If we stay, we're lost for certain. If we escape, we have hope. Not certainty, but hope.' He cupped her face in his hands tenderly and stared deep into her eyes. 'I want you to write your book. I want to be with Kalzamond of Dome. I want to be part of her story.'

She melted into his embrace, feeling the strength and security there. 'When do we escape?' she whispered.

'Tonight.'

'And now?'

He stroked her hair gently, 'We'll prepare for tonight, have a large meal, then you'll rest. You can have the bed again.'

'It's okay it's your turn, or we could share it,' said Kallie, softly.

'But...'

'Don't worry, I meant what I said last night. I intend to sleep, but cuddling you would be nice.'

Chapter 7
Renegades

Kallie's eyes opened very slowly. She was alone in the bed. From under the sheet she hazily peeked out.

Andy sat motionless at his console, which was a blur of information. Only his fingers jerked occasionally to tap keys or hold a page for a moment before the screen returned to the blur.

'You okay?' she mumbled, half-awake. Andy appeared totally unaware of her, as if he was at one with the computers that controlled every aspect of Dome life. Her eyes drifted closed again and she slipped back to sleep.

He was perched on the edge of the bed beside her when she next woke.

'It's getting late,' he said softly. 'We'll be safer now it's dark.'

She nodded in agreement, then sat up and pulled him close in a moment to treasure. She gently kissed the small surgical scar on the nape of his neck then slipped out of bed.

A fresh set of clothes were on the chair for her; his were on the table.

'Did you have to pick such a ghastly colour?' she asked, as she changed from the orange and blue starred pyjamas she had slept in, into the blue-grey cape and tunic he'd picked.

'It will help blend with the shadows,' answered Andy, his tone totally professional. 'I've done a little research into the outer world but I doubt it will help much. A lot of the data is either myth or Council-inspired warnings to keep away. But, I've worked this much out: they can't dispute the logic that says if the farm was totally contaminated, our food would also be deadly. Hence, we would have nothing to eat. Therefore catching radiation is a lie to scare us from escaping.'

Then he continued with a smile, 'What I have also done is to leave a false trail. We're spending a week in the Pleasure Halls. That might give us a few extra days to get further away.'

'Hey, do I look like someone who goes pleasuring?' protested Kallie.

'You do now. I'm a pretty persuasive debater as far as the Council knows and you're an anti-standard student. You'd go there just to be different from the rest of your peers,' joked Andy. He was obviously trying to stop her from worrying by being light-hearted.

'Do you think we'll make it?' asked Kallie, when she had dressed.

'I wouldn't ask you to come with me if I wasn't pretty confident we have a good chance of making it.'

Andy's positive attitude made her feel better and eased the fears she had. She went to him and took him in her arms.

'Andy, whatever happens after tonight, I want you to know I'm trying to escape of my own free choice. I want to go because I don't want Correction or to be someone else. And, I want to be with you. I know I can trust you. You are part of my story now.'

'And you, Kallie, are part of *my* life's story too,' replied Andy, kissing her for the first time. They were more than just friends.

Ten minutes later they were arm in arm outside the residential block, haplessly meandering along but heading towards the edge. Kallie noticed a Guardian enter the far end of the street. It would sense two drunken intoxicators wandering home from the entertainment complex. It went into Andy's building; she knew in a few minutes it would report from Andy's residence that it had failed to arrest its targets.

Concerned the Guardian would decide to question the drunks, she hurried Andy to get themselves well out of sight. If it scanned the area fruitlessly it would have to begin a systematic search, which would give them precious time.

'What's beyond this barrier?' Kallie asked cautiously. They had reached an eight-foot-high wire mesh fence.

'It's called Service Zone One,' Andy replied. 'Beyond here are the power receivers, converters, catalogue warehouses, climate control outlets and countless other things that need to be topside.'

'Oh,' she said, trying to sound as if she understood.

Andy climbed up and straddled the barrier, assisted her over then dropped down beside her. 'If we're seen now, acting won't help It's an RO area.'

'Robots Only, eh?' repeated Kallie. 'How far is it across?' She looked around at the strange buildings and equipment that stretched out in all directions.

'About a mile straight ahead,' Andy answered.

'Okay, let's go. This place gives me the creeps.'

They made their way from shadow to shadow, round ducts, pipes and humming control units. The lighting was sparse, just sufficient for the older Vox robots that worked there. One passed at a distance, unable to detect human presence, being neither equipped adequately nor alerted to the need.

Some while later, Kallie stopped suddenly. 'What's that glow?' she whispered nervously.

'The edge of Dome,' Andy whispered back, 'And a real problem.' A few minutes later they had reached the limit of the Service Zone. An open area lay between them and the rim of Dome itself.

'It doesn't reach the ground,' said Kallie in surprise. 'I'd always presumed it did. I thought we were totally enclosed and protected from the outside.' She was crouched behind him looking at the short pillars that supported Dome some seven feet from the ground. Sand and debris was piled against them by the wind that came in under the rim. Occasionally lightning cracked disintegrating bits of rubbish blown between the columns.

'It doesn't have to reach the ground,' explained Andy. 'But it does have to be perfectly level, hence the pillars, and I think air gets in that way before it's sterilised. Sensors must detect other stuff coming in as most of it gets vaporised by protective circuits in the columns.'

'Oh, well,' said Kallie, as she crept round him. 'Shall we go?'

'Careful! Mind the drop.' He pulled her back from the edge of a ledge. 'There may be alarms or traps down there.'

'Oh great, just when I thought the worst was over. What do we do now?' asked Kallie, exasperated and seeing for the first time they were on a ledge.

'We move round and hopefully there will be a path out or a better way down to the ground.' Andy paused. 'Let's hope we're lucky. It's nearly dawn.'

'What's that?'

'Dawn? Oh, that's what they called day-start outside.' He began to walk to his right.

Kallie grabbed his arm. 'No, let's go this way. It feels luckier,' she said, pulling him towards the left. Slowly they made their way along the ledge.

It was a ten or twelve foot drop from the ledge to the ground and some fifty yards across the open space to the rim. The wind below them scattered the sand and debris about aimlessly first one way then the other. It was watching a piece of this that caused Kallie to look back beyond Andy.

'Andy, we're being followed,' she said, horrified at what she saw. The Vox was some way behind them on the same ledge.

'What?' He turned to look back. 'It must have been alerted to us. We have to find a way down soon. The Vox is slow but relentless. We'll tire long before it does.' He pushed Kallie to quicken her pace.

'Andy, up ahead.' She instinctively knew it was what they sought. Some distance away was a long ramp sloping down from the ledge and going out under the rim. They began to run.

Kallie spotted the Guardian on the far side of the ramp as it quickened its pace. She stopped. Andy pushed her to keep going for the ramp.

'We won't make it, Andy. There's a Guardian coming, it'll cut us off.' Her tiredness and fears suddenly overwhelmed her.

'We must try,' yelled Andy, pushing her forward.

She began running again. 'We won't make it,' she repeated fighting back her fears. She could see the Guardian would reach the ramp easily before them.

Kallie slowed and stopped running as the Guardian reached the opposite side of the wide ramp. It had cut off their escape. But it wasn't this that had caused all three of them to stop. It was the noise. It was like nothing she had ever heard before. The low mechanical rumble and grating sound could do them no good; it had the sound of the Council about it.

She half-turned to Andy. 'I'm sorry, Andy. But we tried anyway,' she said, forcing a smile. Andy took her in his arms as she continued, 'Correction Centre or detention, it was worth it.' She sniffed back a tear and whispered, 'I think I was falling in love with you, but we've run out of time. Just hold me these last few moments. I may not remember them tomorrow, but they are worth everything right now.' She held him close, her fears easing as he stroked her hair. She held him like there was no tomorrow, and she knew for them that was true.

Across the Guardian's path a huge, long and low farm drone rumbled slowly onto the slope heading towards the rim. In her mind Kallie thanked it for going outside and giving them these extra last few moments together.

'Outside; it's going outside!' The thought echoed round Kallie's mind. There was no time to ask Andy about anything, the drone was virtually past them. There wasn't even time to think. She just dragged Andy and they tumbled over the edge. As they hit the sandy ground it felt strange, soft, loose and it moved under their feet as they got up. 'Grab onto the drone,' shouted Kallie.

They ran, they stumbled, they fell and got up again and finally they reached the ramp as the drone slowly rumbled past in front of them.

'Just hang on to anything,' Kallie screamed above the noise. She didn't know if she was screaming at Andy or herself. She grabbed a pipe and a bracket-like protrusion and hauled herself onto something that looked like a wheel protector. Andy found handholds and pulled himself up a little way back from where she clung on to the drone.

They both hung on as it trundled the last few metres to the rim. They hung on as the electrostatic shields cracked all around them as the drone passed under the rim. They hung on as the noise rose in pitch until the drone sped along like a subway train. Not even the Guardian could pursue them at this pace.

Kallie knew that at the top of the ramp the Vox would report the confusion of movement it had detected. The Guardian would evaluate the facts and begin probing the area below. It would find nothing! Eventually the Vox would return to its duties and the Guardian would report yet another failed objective and await fresh directives.

The farm drone came to a rapid halt deep into the farm itself. Kallie dropped, exhausted, from the side and stumbled clear; Andy followed. She stood there, unable to take it all in. There was so much green vegetation, the like of which she could never have imagined before.

'What now?' she asked.

'What do you suggest?' replied Andy, 'You're the one with inspiration.'

'Is that controlled by the Council?' asked Kallie, pointing at the drone now working away, oblivious of them or its part in their escape.

Andy nodded. 'And that,' he said pointing to silver-grey Dome in the far distance.

'Then let's go this way.' She turned her back on both. 'Is this stuff safe?' she asked, going towards the field of green. 'The whole place smells weird.'

'I think it's safe. I think it's food before the Council process it.' Andy replied.

'But it's so green,' she said, nervously stepping into the waist-high plants. Then she laughed. 'Not my colour at all, is it?'

Kallie led the way at first, fascinated by all she saw and taking in the odours that wafted past her nose. The plants had a different smell from the soil, which in turn smelt unlike the air. As the sun rose higher in the sky she began to sweat; it was hotter than the weather inside Dome, where every day was a comfortable 25 degrees. Then a slight breeze picked up; it cooled her down and brought even newer aromas her way. She chatted constantly at first, speculating about things she spotted or the purpose of the ditches they had to get across. Once she got over being scared of insects she happily swatted them whenever they approached her.

'Andy! What's that?' she cried, suddenly realising the empty field they were now in wasn't empty after all. The large brown boulder she had decided was a pile of earth had got up onto four thin legs and turned an ugly-looking face towards her. It had pointed ears and two more pointed things a bit like teeth but growing out of its skull. Underneath its stomach hung a large pink bag-like growth that must have been painful.

'I've no idea Kallie, but I think we have found the source of the nasty smell you said was here.'

'Is it a dangerous animal? The sort we read about in vidi-books as children?' she asked, looking round the field and seeing dozens and dozens more of the earth mounds.

'I hope not,' said Andy. 'Just the same we'd best move to the edge of the field, then if they come for us we can escape across the ditch.'

Kallie let Andy lead after that. 'What do you think that animal is called?' she asked once they were safely walking alongside the ditch again.

'I'll call it a Mooz because that's the sound it made,' replied Andy.

They kept trekking towards the horizon, which Andy said would take them further away from Dome's transmitter range even if their route wasn't perfectly straight.

Five hours later they sat on the banks of an irrigation channel and ate the food Andy had brought. It was cold, but Kallie was past caring. For a while she toyed with the empty containers and mud, and then fell asleep exhausted. She was just too tired to cross another ditch.

Chapter 8
Zak

'Greetings Father, I trust you are well?' said Ben warmly, as the door before him opened.

'Hello, son, thanks for asking. I've not too many aches today, but my bones tell me that it is autumn and winter is just around the corner,' replied the old Gatherer, who had opened the door to Ben's knock. 'I didn't expect to see you so soon after the bonding,' he added, whilst obviously pleased to see his boy.

'Father, I've brought Zak to see you because I want you to hear what she told me yesterday, when we were by the lake.'

Ben had said he would take Zak to his father's quarters under the terraces because Tela was the tribe's Senior Elder and he also knew more than anyone else did about Crazyman and tribal ways. Tela's shoulder-length grey hair and bush of a beard hid most of his leathery-skinned face and though he was not as agile as he once was, his sharp hazel eyes were always alive and bright. He was wrapped in a long, brown, cowhide coat that opened at the front to reveal his blue tee-shirt and black slacks.

'Come in, come in, you two lovebirds,' said Tela. He grinned mischievously at Zak. 'Is that boy of mine's imagination running away with him again?

What is it this time? Has he dreamt you're with child already?'

Chuckling softly, Ben's father backed into his lower room, letting them both enter the long chamber he had created behind the old sport shop's front counter, shutter and door. There was an oval wooden table and several seats taken from the terraces as furniture. Light was provided by a single oil lamp set among the bric-a-brac and crockery on the table, whilst the outside terracing produced a sloping back wall that had a few sacks full of food and vegetables stacked against it. A ladder to the bedroom above them stood in one corner and reflection in a large glass mirror helped brighten the dark cubby-hole of a home.

'Take a seat, Zak,' chirped Tela, folding down the front of one by the table. 'And you, Ben. Now, would you like a drink? I've fruit juice or some honey mead.'

'It's okay Father,' said Ben, taking a seat next to Zak. 'We won't disturb you for long. It's just that Zak had this amazing dream the other night and I think you should hear about it. It could be very important.'

'It was nothing, Ben,' insisted Zak, 'just a crazy dream about Crazyman.'

Tela's eyes sparkled at the name. 'Why not let me decide?' he replied, taking a seat in front of them both. 'If it is nothing, I'll gladly say. But if it's important, then the tribe should be told.' His craggy face broke into a warm smile. He wasn't old in years, perhaps forty-six summers, but tribal life had taken its toll. The hard work and exposed living had aged his body. 'And remember this,' added Tela, 'I knew Crazyman, so I should be able to give a good interpretation of what you say.'

'I had this dream the night before last,' said Zak, hesitantly retelling her dream to Tela. 'It was so real, it was like it was actually happening. I was there, listening to Crazyman telling stories. Ben said he knew them and that I must have heard them somewhere, too. But I swear they were new to me.

'Then there was a tale neither of us had heard about fire, water, earth and the air being our friends. Crazyman was telling it to me. I was just a child, I know that and there were lots of other children with me. He talked to us all but it was like I was the only one who could hear everything he was saying. The other children tried and tried but they kept missing bits. They missed the bits about the towers – twin towers that support Dome – being all wrapped up in the story. I heard him say that many times and that without them Dome would fall.

'Then when it was dying down, I got up and put more wood on his fire for him. He smiled at me, just me, and said that I was a clever girl and the one who would find the way to take us home. He said I was the one who would find the way and we could all go back to Dome.

'I was really proud of myself as I stood in front of him. I kept thinking, me, I will find the way, and he kept saying it too. I would find the way. I would find the way. Again and again we said it. Then I woke up.' Zak fell silent.

'You see, Father,' said Ben, 'she's the one who will find the way to get back into Dome and free the citizens, so we can all survive.'

'But Ben,' said Zak, 'I don't know how to get back into Dome. Getting out all but killed me. It was luck. I don't believe I could find a way back, let alone free the citizens there.' Her head sank, showing her disappointment for not being able to do what Ben wished.

'There, there, Zak,' said Tela kindly. 'Don't let it upset you. Ben has always been impatient.' He turned to his son.

'Look at me, Ben. I am just a little over forty-six years of age, yet my body is like that of an oldie inside Dome. The tribe cannot survive forever in the ruins, it takes too much of a toll. Children need educating better and nowadays new Renegades are rare. We have to find a way to benefit from the Council's abilities, without being enslaved by them. But we won't do it by pressurising Zak. We have freedom of choice. The price we are paying is short lives, just as Crazyman predicted. He also predicted victory, and it will come. But it will come in its own good time.'

'But surely Father, if Zak stayed with you and the Elders she could learn more about Dome and then work out how to find a way in?'

'Oh Ben, do you forget she was the last Renegade to survive long enough to reach the tribe? Zak knows Dome as well as any of us. It never changes. There is no choice there, Ben. No freedom to be yourself, no development of an individual, only The Way of Dome. If a person doesn't comply with standard behaviour, then their flaws are corrected and they become a new citizen who fits into their place in Dome's society.' Tela turned his attention to Zak once more. 'Tell me, Zak, my dear, what was Crazyman sitting on?'

Puzzled for a second, Zak thought for a moment. 'I don't know,' she replied. 'It seemed as though he sat on the ground – but wait, he was actually sitting on an old tree stump. Yes, that's right because I got part of the same fallen tree for his fire.'

'Then don't worry yourself any more. If you are to find the way it will come to you. If you don't, the tribe is no worse today than it was before your dream.'

'But Father, it was the night we bonded,' Ben protested. 'A woman's night of certain truth, everyone knows that.'

'Ben, be patient,' pleaded Tela. 'If it is to be it shall be. Now go gathering as you should. Let the matter rest.'

Ben agreed to do that and they left Tela nursing his thoughts of Crazyman's last days with the tribe. In those days he had sat on his old tree stump, not on the ground, and he told tales to the children, few as they were. But he would also scold them for not stoking the fires. Ben's father smiled to himself. Maybe, just maybe; there was always hope.

Ben and Zak gathered into the day, then, towards noon, rested on the banks of an irrigation ditch. Zak lay watching the clouds, her head cradled in Ben's lap.

'Ben,' said Zak lazily, 'are we going to survive to have children?'

'You better believe it,' he replied, idly twisting her plaits. 'We'll have lots of them. So long as we avoid the farm drones and keep clear of the Guardians there's nothing to stop us.'

'In Dome, every Domer is guaranteed a child; we can have one each to keep the population standard size. And there aren't any problems due to poor diet or lack of medicine if children get sick. And of course, the Council sends oldies to the Hospice to spend their final days when they reach one hundred and ten. They say that is fair and The Way of Dome.' She sighed, thinking of how some aspects of Dome life were good. 'I'll try to find the way back into Dome but I've no idea where to start looking.' She squeezed his muscular arm fondly. 'Dome sits on short pillars. I figure a couple of them must be the two towers Crazyman talked about. But I don't know how to work out which pair doesn't have the electrostatic protection wall.'

'The what?'

'The wall of lightning. Anything that goes under the rim is hit by a lightning bolt, except I guess, between the two towers Crazyman talked about.'

'You must have come through there, that's obvious – otherwise you'd have been killed.'

'No. When I reached the rim I fell off a ledge and was knocked unconscious. When I came round it was dark. As the wind blew things under the rim, the flashes frightened me so much I couldn't move. I just lay there, scared stiff. Slowly I realised what I was seeing and how it worked to protect Dome. Sensors spot something and flash generators blast it. But I also noticed if two things went under together, the second one sometimes made it through, especially if it was off the ground. I made the second big decision of my life there and then. I threw the biggest piece of debris I could manage into the gap and dived after it. It felt like every bone in my body jarred but I landed on the outside. That's how desperate I was to escape. I would have rather died than go back to The Way of Dome.'

'Wow! If that was the second biggest decision, what was your first?' Ben was engrossed; Zak rarely spoke about her life inside Dome.

'My first ever big decision was to escape. You were born out here, so you will never fully understand. You have always had choice. Choice based on reasons of your own. If you want something you choose it and know the reasons why you made that decision.' Her voice became cold. 'In Dome the Council decides who you are and what you want. They don't even bother to tell you the reasons why. You cannot choose to be different or someone who doesn't fit their standard Dome criteria. Everything you need is provided and you are told you want for nothing. So the citizens believe it is true because they live in blissful ignorance.

'Then one day you realise you don't want the life that's been planned for you. You want something different. That wanting gnaws away inside you day and night until you have to do something you've never done before. You choose without asking the Council's permission. I wanted to be clever in standard education, but I wasn't. Learning wasn't easy for me. I studied hard but I couldn't seem to understand the way other students did. Vocationship was just a vague hope for me. I wanted Art; a want I could never make happen.

'Then the Council chose my career path two years early. I was to be a serving wench in the Pleasure Halls. I was only just into womanhood when I was apprenticed there. The place is repulsive. I was told over the next few years I would learn how to please professionals. My eventual profession was to be an object of their gratification and lust.

'During my first week I had to wash people's hot, sweaty bodies after they had *enjoyed* themselves. It was sickening; I hid throughout the next week and ran away on my third. Anything would be better, even death.'

Zak bitterly looked away, focusing on nothing – but then on something across the muddy water in the opposite field. 'Ben, what's that?' she asked, urgently.

'Oh shit,' he whispered. 'It's another Guardian.' He twisted, letting her head slide from his lap. 'Zak, slowly get back up the bank and into the field. It won't have sensed us yet; at least I hope not.'

They both slid up into the field and hid among the vegetables. Across the canal the Guardian moved towards them, slowly and systematically scanning the area around it. It stopped, probed and scanned again. They knew it could not cross the water so they felt safe. Then, without warning, a laser blast ripped into the field and their cart exploded in flames.

The Guardian scanned again, then, instead of seeking a bridge, it began to slowly climb down the bank opposite Ben and Zak.

'Ben, it's not avoiding the water any more. We'd better move and quick.'

The Guardian heard them and fired a blast that was too high.

'Run!' Ben yelled.

The Guardian slowly waded across the ditch and climbed the other bank in pursuit. They ran, leaving criss-cross trails through the tall vegetation, and crossed two further ditches hoping they would slow the Guardian down.

Arching a path across the fields, they breathlessly came to the widest ditch. 'We'll have to cross here and then make for the perimeter, 'Ben panted. 'Let's hope it can't go beyond the boundaries of the farm.' Hand in hand they leapt over the edge and slid towards the water below.

Before they reached it there was a startled scream and Zak thumped into an unexpected obstruction.

Chapter 9
The Ditch

Kallie screamed as she was sent sprawling like a discarded rag doll into the muddy water several feet below.

Andy heard Kallie's scream and spun round in an instant from where he'd been resting to see two girls tumbling, like Chinese fighting kites, headlong into the ditch.

He caught a second movement from the corner of his eye and lunged out with an arm. He managed to grab the collar of the coat of someone sliding past, precariously close to knocking him into the ditch in the same way that Kallie had been. Something had gone seriously wrong with their escape and it took him a few seconds to realise they had been leapt upon by two strangers. Andy dragged the lad he had got hold of, who was now kicking, twisting and yelling, back up the embankment.

The lad swung a clenched fist wildly in the direction of Andy's arm; Andy blocked it easily. He tried to punch again, this time at the face in front of him, from the kneeling position he had managed to get into. The blow was turned away effortlessly by Andy as he dragged the lad to his side. A powerful arm locked around the boy's neck and the blocked arm was pulled back against its joint.

'Let me go, you idiot, or I'll rip your head off,' screamed the lad.

Andy's arm tightened; his captive choked and struggled but it was useless.

'You'd need the strength of a robot to do that,' replied Andy. 'And... What about First Law? A robot can't harm a Domer.' He released his hold and offered his hand in friendship. 'I'm Andy. I've just escaped from Dome.'

The lad took the hand with a smile and said, 'I'm Ben, and I live out here.'

Below, knee deep in the muddy water, Kallie staggered to her feet to see someone on all fours in front of her. From what she saw she believed they had been discovered by a Super Vox. Instinct and confusion told her she had to do something. The Super Vox was the Council's latest humanoid robot. It had all the features of a real Domer: texturised skin, real hair and various facial expressions. They were also allowed to wear clothes but had to be bare-chested, or, in the case of female models, have nothing but a modesty strip across their tops when in public.

Like any Domer, the most violent Kallie had ever got before was to use insult, sarcasm, criticism or personal slur. There was never any physical force used by Domers; that was the exclusive province of the Guardians – until now. The flash of bare skin from the missing panel in the torn tunic convinced Kallie that to remain free she had to deal with a Super Vox. Lunging awkwardly forward, she sent her opponent headlong into the mire. Jumping onto its back she tried to hold the head under the surface hoping the water would damage its circuitry.

The robot then recovered from crashing into Kallie, arched upwards and twisted, throwing her off. It lunged out and grabbed a fistful of auburn hair, wrapped it round its wrist and pulled hard. Kallie screamed again, this time in pain. Her agonised yell was silenced by a mouthful of muddy water as she sprawled face down in the ditch. She took hold of the arm dragging her through the dirty stream and bit it as hard as she could.

'Ouch, you brat!' screamed the humanoid robot, slapping Kallie's face. Kallie responded by clambering to her knees and swinging an arm to hit its exposed side. It let go of Kallie's hair. Kallie staggered to her feet. An arm swung around Kallie's neck then a leg slammed into the back of her knees. Kallie tumbled backwards. She twisted as she fell, ripping her tunic from her shoulder and arm to expose bare flesh and a green bra. It was now Kallie who was on all fours in the muddy waters. She felt a stamp in the centre of her back that sent her sprawling spread-eagled face down. With a foot on her spine she kicked and floundered desperately until the robot straddled her and pushed her face into the shallow muddy water. Her hair was pulled back then her face smacked into the mud again and again.

'Stop! Please stop, you're hurting me,' gasped Kallie between the thrusts. She started to cry. The side of her face hit the mud one more time and stayed there. The pressure on her back eased and she was twisted by her hair to face the sky. She saw who had beaten her so easily sitting on her chest. It was another girl. 'Who are you?' Kallie sobbed.

'I'll ask the questions,' snapped the girl. 'Identify yourself.'

'Student Kalzamond 486 of Sector 15, Citizen,' sobbed Kallie, automatically answering the demand. She wiped the mud from her face with her free hand.

'Oh!' said the girl, clearly not being accustomed to that form of address from someone about her own age. She moved off and sat beside Kallie. 'I thought you were a robot but now I can see you're fully dressed. Besides I guess I wouldn't have beaten you if you were. And robots don't cry, do they?' she added.

'I thought *you* were a robot, too. Who are you and where are you from?' asked Kallie.

'I'm called Zak. Ben, that's my husband, and I are Renegades of Dome,' said the girl with pride.

Seemingly oblivious to their situation, sitting in a dirty muddy ditch, they introduced themselves formally and in a few seconds swapped information. Kallie told Zak how she and Andy had just escaped from Dome and Zak told her about being part of the Renegade tribe and getting married to Ben.

Andy had released Ben and they'd sat watching the girls fight. They had both quickly understood that they were not threats to each other.

Ben smiled proudly at Zak's victory but his grin suddenly gave way to horror as a dark ominous shadow fell across him and Andy. Just above them the Guardian had arrived and was now aiming at the two girls in the water below. Ben's reactions were instant: he leapt upwards and grabbed the robot's arm. The laser blast that followed was wide of its mark by just inches. The residual heat burned Kallie's bare shoulder. Ben clung to the robot's arm but he was no match for the machine. Ignoring its burden the robot began to take aim for a second time.

Andy's full weight hit it from behind and took it off balance. The Guardian toppled into the ditch, Andy fell awkwardly onto the bank, and Ben was sprawled full-length into the water.

'Ben!' screamed Zak. The Guardian had already staggered to its feet with its back to the girls. She saw Ben freeze and the robot's raised arm taking aim directly at him. He was only a few feet in front of it.

Kallie leapt forward and grabbed hold of the Guardian around its domed head, her legs gripping its torso. It barely noticed her weight. Then its arm lowered away from its aim towards Ben, it shook, and took aim again. The machine twitched, lowered its arm once more, whirred then repeated the cycle. Kallie slid down the Guardian's back leaving the ali-foil container firmly stuck with mud wrapped around the microwave signal antenna on the back of its head.

Between them Andy and Ben managed to rip the plastic protective skin on the Guardian and tip it over. It fizzed and died as water flooded in.

Kallie almost cried again as Zak dressed the wound on her arm. The two couples spent some time on the embankment getting over the ordeal, and then Ben invited Andy and Kallie to the ruins to meet the rest of the Renegade tribe.

Chapter 10
The Tribe

It was late in the afternoon by the time the four of them reached the ruins of the pre-Dome town and its derelict stadium where the Renegade tribe lived. Tela welcomed the newcomers with a smile, handshakes, and a big hug for Kallie.

Kallie and Andy didn't argue when Zak suggested they should share her and Ben's shelter for their first nights. They could find their own place to live once they were settled.

Ben, like a few other members of the tribe, lit a fire in the wide porch-like area between the outside and open space inside the stadium and set about making a meal. He explained that natural air flow from what were once the exit gates took smoke out through the stairwells that led to the terraces.

Kallie stared in awe. She thought Ben starting his fire with a flint and file was amazing. The meat he then dropped into the big pot of water once it was boiling just couldn't be believed. Until that moment Kallie had never related meat to living things; she'd only ever seen pictures of outer-world creatures in vidi-books. Ben explained to her a chicken was a bird of some sort. He cut it into several pieces and stirred the bits into what he referred to as a stew. She was astonished at the way he stood at his table and chopped up what he called vegetables.

Food only ever came in small manageable cubes in Dome; Ben's was all sorts of shapes and sizes. He then took some powder-like stuff, added water and fat to make something he called dumplings. Kallie stared on in wonder.

If Andy was equally enthralled his face didn't show it. He looked on in interest and watched intently, as if taking everything in, perhaps for future reference.

'Hey, come on you two,' laughed Zak. 'I want to take you around our home. Ben will be some time yet, he's still got the spices to add. It'll be light for another hour and there's a lot to see. There's loads of stuff I want to show you.'

'But this is fascinating,' said Kallie, pointing to the bubbling cauldron.

'I know, but Ben or I do it every day so it's lost its fascination for us,' joked Zak. 'Come on Andy, I'm sure there are many things here you'll both find even more incredible and interesting.' She turned to Ben and said, 'We'll be back by the time it is done, my husband. Oh, and see if you can barter some mead from the neighbours along the alley. Use some of the bread I baked yesterday.'

Ben looked up and smiled broadly. 'Yeah; okay, that's a brilliant idea Zak; we're going to have a great evening.' He returned his attention to rolling the dough into bite-size balls ready to drop into his stew-pot.

Zak led Kallie and Andy out of the stadium and onto a street lined on either side with derelict buildings of various shapes and sizes. Most were just piles of rubble or burnt-out shells but occasionally one or two would have several of their walls still standing. Kallie could see that many of the buildings had vegetation growing up through their stonework and others were obviously used by the Renegades because they were lit by candles and had been turned into homes with furniture and other things visible through the windows. As they walked rubble-strewn roads, Zak introduced the new arrivals to other Renegades of the tribe. Everyone was very pleased to meet them just because they were newcomers and often disappeared into their homes only to return a few minutes later with a gift of food or clothing. Kallie was really surprised at this; presents were not the norm in Dome.

'This is our store pit,' said Zak, at the front of one of the bombed-out buildings. 'Follow me and I'll show you my and Ben's supplies.' She clambered over some of the rubble to a cleared space inside an old residence and stood at the side of a hatchway in the floor of a now defunct room.

'This is where Ben and I keep our gatherings,' she announced proudly and pulled up the trapdoor. She climbed down the cellar steps and motioned for Kallie and Andy to follow. It was cold and dark but dry in the underground room. Zak reached into the darkness, struck a spark, lit a straw taper and then a crudely-made candle. There was now enough light for Kallie to see the place was chock-a-block with boxes, sacks, and all sorts of containers filled to the brim with different vegetables. Some were sealed to be airtight; others had wet sacks over them, whilst still more were just left in the cool of the room.

'What's all this?' asked Andy, as his eyes became accustomed to the gloom. His voice had a slight echo in the void.

'All Gatherers have a store pit or place to keep the fruit and vegetables they get from the farm,' answered Zak. 'Then once a week we take some of it to the big pitch for others to have.'

'You mean you give it away?' queried Andy, sounding surprised.

'No,' said Zak sounding bemused. 'The Elders have a law that says we must share everything we gather or hunt with everyone in the tribe. Ben and I gather and store for the tribe, not ourselves. We let other members of the tribe have what we've collected and in return we get other vegetables, fruit, flour and extra food items we need. Hunters distribute meat every other day but you have to let them know what you want. They give you enough for a few days.'

'Is it like a service unit? Where you can get anything you want but from other people on the big pitch?' asked Kallie, sort of recognising the process.

'Not quite; you can't get *anything*. There are lots of things you had in Dome we don't have. But we've got everything we need.'

Zak snuffed out the candle and they climbed back into the late afternoon sun. She took them off in another direction showing them various landmarks of the town and the entrances to the big pitch of the stadium.

'There are a lot of old rusting metal things around,' said Andy, pointing to several items they passed, 'What are they?'

'I don't really know,' answered Zak. 'Some look like burned-out auto cabs and there's steel work from buildings and the like, but it's the smaller things that are the most useful. We use those bits as materials if we need to make something.'

'You make stuff?' said Kallie, once again surprised.

'Of course we do,' laughed Zak. 'Ben and his brother made our cart. Mind you, we're going to have to make a new cart tomorrow but Ben's already found some wheels. We have to do everything for ourselves; I searched out our plates and cutlery. I found them in a house that had been destroyed. There are no service units, robots or drones out here, and definitely no Guardians.'

'But how did you learn to make things? Did it take a lot of debating?' asked Andy. He seemed as fascinated by the concept as Kallie was. 'How do you know things will work?'

'Oh, that's easy,' replied Zak. 'In the early days Crazyman –, he was our founder – and others went shop raiding and house hunting. They found all sorts of useful things like our candles and firelighters. They were originally much smaller but the file and flint is the same principle. There was loads of clever stuff from the people who used to live here. Some of the smarter Renegades ingeniously worked out what things did and just copied how they worked.'

'What if someone can't make stuff, hunt or gather food?' asked Andy. He seemed to be getting the idea of how the tribe worked.

'You mean like the older members of the tribe, or the children? The Elders usually speak to a few of the parents and ask them to look after others instead of hunting or gathering for the tribe. Everybody has to contribute in some way to tribal life. Also, if you have a skill you can barter for things. Enan made us an oven so we can bake and swap the bread and cakes for things we don't have, like the mead I asked Ben to get. Having said that I guess it's time we headed back, don't you?'

Looking around her Kallie could see how everyone they met, though rugged, grubby and tired, looked content.

Back at the shelter they sat at a table and ate Ben's chicken stew with dumplings and bread.

'Ben, your food is awkward to eat but delicious,' said Kallie, chewing on a chicken bone for the first time in her life.

'Thanks,' said Ben, looking pleased with himself.

'I let Ben do most of the cooking,' said Zak. 'He's better at it than me; but my skills are catching him up,' she added. 'You've never cooked have you? Not to worry, you can eat with us for a few days and we'll show you the basics. Then you can do it for yourselves.'

'Thanks,' said Andy. 'I wondered how we were going to adapt to the changes that are going to be needed.'

'I want to have a go at making the fire,' said Kallie enthusiastically.

'All in good time,' said Ben, with a laugh. 'All in good time. We don't want you burning the place down in your first days here.'

That evening they sat with the tribal Elders around one of the communal fires in the big pitch area. They told of their escape from Dome and their adventures on the farm. Everyone listened with delight at their exploits. Kallie realised that swapping stories was a favourite evening pastime for many of the Renegades.

'Will you stay?' someone asked.

'I won't be going back,' laughed Kallie, 'I promise you that.'

'It will take some getting used to,' added Andy. 'In Dome, infants don't leave the Children Centres to live with one of their parents until they're ten years old... I mean, ten summers,' he corrected himself, using the tribal term. 'Here they grow up with both parents in their shelters and the older folk, not Vox robots, teach them what they need to know.'

'But you have no service units,' said Kallie. 'My clothes are filthy and my back's cold.'

'Here,' said Zak, wrapping her own coat round Kallie's shoulders. 'This time of year the days are usually hot but nights can get quite cold. Tomorrow I'll teach you how to wash your tunic. It will be another first for you.' Everyone roared with laughter.

Ben took a burning branch to kindle the fire back at their dwelling and said, 'Don't be too long Zak, it seems you and Kallie would talk all night given the chance.'

A voice from the far side of the fire called out, 'There's a newly-bonded for you.' Laughter once again rang out into the night.

Zak smiled shyly, the night and her dark skin hiding the blush of her cheeks. She stood up and followed Ben.

Kallie and Andy said goodnight to everyone and followed her.

'Come on, Kallie. Can't waste our day off, the sun is already high.'

Kallie opened her eyes to see Zak's smiling face.

'Ben and Andy went off early to make a new cart, and then they're going pole fishing. We'll head for the lake too when you're ready. We have the washing to do.'

Less than an hour later the two girls were by the lake. Kallie had never seen so much water. It stretched for miles in all directions. She could just make out the cliff face on the far bank through the heat haze. To her right she could see how the two hilly shores swept together smoothly but to her left the water went on and on, disappearing round a rocky outcrop.

'Hey Kallie, come on, don't be frightened. It's lovely!' Zak was already stripped off and waist-deep in the lake enjoying the swirl of the crystal clear water on her skin.

Kallie knew there was no backing down. Sooner or later she would have to wade in. She took a deep breath, slipped out of her tunic and stepped cautiously into the lake. As the water got deeper it felt strange, cool, scary and wet, but not as terrifying as she had imagined.

'Bring your tunic then,' called Zak, now swimming towards her. Kallie returned for the washing and waded back in. Zak swam away to a rocky island a few yards out. She sat on a small, twin-layered bamboo raft tied there with her legs dangling in the water. The raft gently bobbed up and down. She giggled at Kallie's awkward way of getting through the water.

'Can't you swim?' she asked with a smile.

'No. I've never been in so much water before,' replied Kallie. 'You know what Dome is like. There are fountains, ponds and ornamental waterfalls but nothing on this scale.'

'Ben taught me; I'll try and teach you,' encouraged Zak. 'But it's first things first with the tribe: the washing.'

Washing proved not only successful but enjoyable too. Once finished they spread their now clean laundry out on the rocks to dry. Being Dome-manufactured clothing, everything would be wearable quite rapidly. Whilst waiting they splashed and jumped around in fits of giggles and laughter.

Kallie found learning to swim frustrating and difficult though tremendous fun. She swore if she swallowed any more water the lake would dry up.

Zak collapsed with laughter at the suggestion.

'Let's rest a bit,' she said, swimming back to the raft and climbing onto it.

Kallie followed her at her fastest paddle wade.

Moments later Zak had retrieved their dry clothes and stored them safely in the box at the centre of the raft behind the short mast. She then slipped her lower body back into the water and started kicking with her legs to push the raft towards Kallie.

Lunging forward, Kallie swam her first ever three strokes then made a grab for the raft to join Zak. She found being half in the water and half out of it on the raft a much easier way of getting about.

After they had climbed back onto the raft and dressed they lazed in the sun.

'This is nice,' said Kallie, feeling the warm sun on her face. 'How did you get the weather so good on a rest day?'

'I didn't, the weather just happens naturally out here,' replied Zak, equally relaxed.

'Sorry, so much has happened I forget things at times. This is so good,' Kallie sighed. 'I expected to be dead or in the Correction Centre by now. Instead, I'm here having a wonderful time. Thanks, Zak. If I had known what life was like outside, I'd have escaped a long time ago. I think a lot of Domers would.'

'It's not all fun you know. There's work tomorrow and these days there are the huge farm machines to avoid as well as armed Guardians,' murmured Zak.

'How come they attack people? I thought robotic law forbade it.'

'Huh, that's inside Dome,' said Zak. 'A robot must not harm a human or through inaction allow a human to be harmed. Ben reckons the Council must have changed the laws, and out here Renegades don't count as human.'

'Can the Council do that?'

'I don't know; I never had to think about it before.'

'I'll have to ask Andy, he might know.'

'He's nice,' said Zak, 'Does he really know lots?'

'He's a full citizen with a science profession so he must know tons of things,' replied Kallie.

'You have a citizen companion, wow! Isn't he a bit old for you?' queried Zak.

'No, well, I don't think so. We only met a few days ago but he seems to be the perfect companion for me. We get on so well.'

'You must really like his company to have escaped with him, so I guess you would think he's perfect.'

'Sometimes I think he's too perfect for me. Don't you think that about Ben? After all you bonded with him.'

'Oh, Ben's not perfect but for me he's so right. He even thought that I'd find a way for the tribe to get into Dome and replace the Council, like Crazyman predicted they would. I was so embarrassed.'

'Wouldn't that be wonderful if it happened? But how could it?'

'Oh, Crazyman said it was to do with the towers that support Dome. I dreamt about it on our bonding night and Ben's convinced I'll know which two would make Dome collapse.'

'When we escaped I saw that Dome sits on little towers,' said Kallie slowly, with her eyes still closed. 'If we took two of them out and it collapsed, we could march in and take over.'

'I remember them. But, if Dome collapsed, then everyone inside would be killed. And how would we deal with the Guardians who protect Dome?'

'Good point, Zak. I'll ask Andy, he might know. I've only got inspiration and good guesses. He's the one who has the logical solutions to problems...' Kallie's voice trailed off.

'I just keep working at things,' mumbled Zak to herself. 'I wish I could find the way. How do we take the two towers that support Dome?' Her eyelids closed and she too slipped into an afternoon doze.

'Zak! Zak, where's the shore?'

Zak woke suddenly to Kallie's yelling. They had drifted a long way out; their little raft was caught in the south current and was being dragged rapidly away from the safety of the beach near their ruins.

Chapter 11
The Waterwall

Ben found pole fishing an ideal way of relaxing. It had all the peace and quiet he needed to lift the daily anxiety of the Renegade tribe's battle for survival. Anchored not too far from shore, with nothing more than a moderate swell to gently roll his raft on its floats, he could empty his mind and lose himself in the hypnotic bobbing of his rod and line. Then he would get the sudden adrenalin rush that always hit when his float disappeared beneath the crystal clear water, dragged by the urgency of desperate escape that was never to be, as his supper took the bait. That began another conflict, an encounter which made it all worthwhile.

For Andy on the other hand, the process was irrational and non-productive. He had not managed to hook a single fish all afternoon, compared to the half-dozen Ben had already pulled out of the lake.

Ben had acquired his pole from his father who, in his youth along with Crazyman, had scavenged all over the ruins in order to obtain useful items from what was once clearly a thriving little town and whose rubble they now called home. The fibreglass rod whipped nicely and sent his weight and bait far out into the water. In the retail outlet where the two foragers had found all manner of fishing tackle was a poster that demonstrated how the things they discovered could be used.

Andy's borrowed pole was Renegade-made, much heavier and far less flexible; however, like Ben's, the line was only just a little short of being smooth string. Ben explained that the Fishers had the best lightweight yarns and would have a multitude of floats cast out from their rafts. They could land thirty or forty good-size fish in a morning.

Ben taught Andy to cast a line and after a short while Andy managed to cast almost as far as his tutor.

Their raft was a mid-sized craft about ten feet by five feet, constructed from several ten-litre oil drums lashed to a frame, with a deck made of scavenged doors and wooden sheets Ben had searched out. In the centre was a ten-foot mast to which a triangular sail was tied, point to the top. The lower corners could be attached to fixing points on either side if they wanted to use it. Behind this was a bench from which they could paddle through the water.

They were anchored about a hundred yards out from the muddy beach that was edged by scrubland and a few bushes and trees that had re-established themselves in the waste land surrounding their home. They were quite some way down from the girls, who were screened from them by a rocky outcrop. They fished and chatted. Ben quickly realised that Andy was smart, despite him not being very adept at the making of the cart earlier.

'The tribe is really a victim of its own success,' remarked Andy, casting his line once more. 'Prior to Crazyman, Renegades were no threat to Dome because you lived alone or, like your parents, in small family groups on the farm and eventually died of starvation or in accidents. Now, fifteen years later, you are organised and live longer. Your women are encouraged to have as many children as they can to perpetuate the clans and with that many mouths to feed you actually upset the efficiency of the farm. Hence, the Council have responded with the armed Guardians. In what – one generation – you've gone from nothing to a force capable of overthrowing the Council itself. Or so you believe.'

'We are a force,' said Ben emphatically, trying to convince Andy he and the other Renegades controlled their own lives. 'Dome is totally wrong for people. It restricts them and forces them to be nothing more than living robots.'

'But, Ben, look at the tribe;' said Andy. 'You're scavengers; you still live from hand to mouth and you have no energy system for lighting, heating, cooking, or any of the other things that are taken for granted in Dome. The tribe needs all that stuff to continue and prosper.'

'Are you saying that the tribe can't survive without going back into Dome and starting a new order?' asked Ben, as he reeled in his line again. 'If you are, I agree with you. We need the things Dome has to offer but not at the price they demand.'

'No, I'm not actually saying that. I'm thinking The Way of Dome and The Way of the Tribe might be incompatible. Maybe it's time to break away from Dome, its farm and its robots. The people who once lived in the ruins must have had a power system; if we could find where it was kept I might be able to use it again. I'm a science professional and energy supply is physics. The problem is, how Dome or we can create the quantity needed is beyond my understanding, but I'd have a go.'

'We can't stay out here forever, we have to go back,' said Ben, casting his line out in a new direction. 'Crazyman said the day will come when you can't tell the people from the robots. Then the citizens will pray for us to set them free,' he continued. 'It is our destiny to liberate Dome and its citizens.'

'Is that the belief of the tribe?'

'Yeah. Believe me, one day you won't be able to tell people and robots apart,' said Ben in response. 'Everything Crazyman said will come true one day, one way or another. He predicted armed Guardians before he died and they are here now.'

'You have never been in Dome, Ben. It's clean, it's airy, and the buildings are fantastic – not broken down like here. Everything you need is there for you as long as you fit into a standard lifestyle. That's the problem. People are easy to see. They have a kind of blankness about them; it's like a hidden pain below the surface. There are very few like Kallie who have that spark of life in them that you know should be there. The citizens mostly live orderly Council-approved lives and debate the same issues that are always debated, reaching the conclusions that are always reached. Oh, yes, there are robots that look like human beings but you can't mistake the two. It's almost as if the individuals have slipped below robot lives. They are sad. They don't have feelings or passions, whereas robots never had them in the first place. Robots don't look as if they have lost something vital to their existence. Domers do. That's why they need to be freed. I really hope the tribe can do it.'

'Then you agree with us Dome needs the tribe and we need them... Hey, you've got a bite,' exclaimed Ben suddenly.

'Have I?' replied Andy in surprise.

'Yeah, strike now, then reel it in gently and you'll land your first fish.' Ben could see the sudden excitement in Andy's eyes as the thrill of what they were doing finally took hold. As Andy wound in his line Ben continued, 'Crazyman said that someone would find the way and overthrow the Council. Couldn't you lead us, Andy? You're strong and smart. If anyone could lead us, you could.'

'What about Zak? You were convinced it would be her yesterday.'

'I know, but she doesn't believe it and now you have arrived. I don't know any more.'

'I'll help all I can but I think you should have faith in your woman,' said Andy, lifting his trophy from the water with a net the way he'd seen Ben do. 'I'll be part of your struggle but I'm only here because of Kallie. Without her, I might not have left

Dome. It was her who inspired me. I trust her intuition and you should trust Zak. Give her time. Have faith, Ben. Faith makes even the impossible possible.'

Ben smiled to himself while Andy sat on the bench admiring his catch. 'You're right; it just seems there is inevitability about everything these days. Somehow, it doesn't always feel right. It's as if we are caught up in something much bigger, much stronger than anyone realises and there is nothing I, or any one person, can do about it. It's like that raft out there caught in the south current. Its fate is sealed. Eventually it will be smashed to pieces on the Waterwall. Nothing can stop that happening.'

'What do you mean, Ben?' asked Andy.

'That raft out there, its destiny is set. It will be smashed on the Waterwall and sucked through the sluice gates to the giant waterfalls the other side.'

'But aren't the girls on that raft?' said Andy, shielding his eyes to see more clearly.

'No! Wait – yeah, that's bad, that's very bad!' gasped Ben, in horror. 'There's no escape from the south current. As soon as you're caught by it you have to dive in and swim like crazy for the shore. Waste five minute trying to save the raft and neither you nor it will escape.'

Before he had finished speaking, Andy had hauled in their anchor and started paddling out to the stricken craft.

'What are we going to do?' Ben asked, anxiously.

'I don't know yet, Ben,' Andy replied, pulling hard with his paddle to close the gap between the rafts. 'I'll think as we go. Now start paddling; remember Kallie and I can't swim.'

Ben grabbed his oar and joined Andy in their pursuit of the other craft.

The girls desperately fought with the current. They lay on either side of their little raft with an arm outstretched pulling at the water with their hands. Zak hadn't bothered to take oars for the washing trip as they weren't meant to stray from the shore. Using their arms was the best she could think of doing.

Kallie looked ahead and saw the other raft heading towards them. She stood up and waved.

'Look!' she yelled above the wind that always blew through the middle of the lake. 'It must be Andy and Ben.'

'We must get closer to the edge of this current,' shouted Zak. 'If they get caught in it we will all be dragged to the Waterwall.'

'The what?' yelled Kallie.

'The Waterwall; it stops the lake flooding the valley and reaching Dome. It's a wall and a giant waterfall.'

Kallie looked back towards Andy and yelled for him to take care. She didn't want them being pulled into the faster current too.

The other raft bobbed precariously close to the faster waters but was still too far away.

'They can't get any closer,' said Kallie, realising they were nowhere near enough. Then she heard a new sound. That of crashing water, and in the distance the harsh lines of the Waterwall appeared. 'Zak, could you swim for it? It's your only chance,' insisted Kallie breathlessly.

'If Ben met me I might make it, but you can't swim.'

'Forget me. I've no hope, but you might just make it clear of the current.'

'I can't leave you, Kallie.'

'Of course you can – if you don't, you'll be killed. We both will,' argued Kallie.

'But there must be something we can do to save us both,' retorted Zak.

'Like what?' yelled Kallie, across the deck. 'This morning you warned me about the dangers of the lake including the south current. You said only a very strong swimmer could escape and I can't swim.'

'You could hold on to me.'

'Look,' Kallie said firmly, 'one or both of us will be dead soon. The tribe needs you more than it needs me. Besides, I've lived two more days than I expected. They were worth it all.' She lay back down and pulled at the lake with all her strength.

Zak perched on the edge of the raft watching the current for a calm eddy or flow. She looked up and called out, 'You had better come and get me, Ben, because then we have to rescue Kallie.'

She looked back at Kallie. Blood trickled from her injured arm as she put all her strength into each pull at the lake. 'I'm doing this for you and me, Kallie,' said Zak. She took a deep breath, then...

The fishing line and weight snaked out from Andy's pole. The line wrapped around their mast. It became taut as Zak leapt up and tied it securely. Ben's line followed, dropping across Kallie's back. Zak grabbed it and knotted it round the mast too.

'What are you doing?' Kallie yelled as Zak joined her. 'Are you crazy?'

'No, I'm not crazy. We're saving ourselves. Ben and Andy have got lines to our raft. If they can tow us and we paddle with them we could get out of this current and into the calm water.'

'Paddling won't work,' said Kallie, sliding backward and halfway off the rear of the raft. She began thrashing with her legs.

'Brilliant idea,' cried Zak, quickly joining her

As they kicked for all their worth, Kallie saw the boys erect their sail and felt the raft begin to swing in a long sweeping arc out of the current and into the calmer waters by the shore.

Chapter 12
The Seer

The girls' raft beached about half a mile back from the Waterwall. They staggered ashore, cold, wet and exhausted. Within seconds Ben and Andy were with them. The relief and joy showed in tears, kisses and hugs.

'Wow, Andy! That was amazing,' enthused Ben, once the joy and elation had subsided a little. 'We've got to get back with this story, you'll be a hero and...'

'Whoa! Before we head back the girls ought to rest a while and dry out a bit,' insisted Andy. 'We've miles to walk before we reach the ruins. Paddling against the currents this close to the Waterwall is not something I'm keen on.'

'Yeah, I suppose you're right,' sighed Ben, calming down a little more. 'We have a fair bit of the afternoon left and they could do with half an hour before we start the hike back.'

Kallie agreed with Andy and the pair of them went to rest on the scrubland that fell away from the muddy beach. She wanted to snuggle up to Andy, who was sitting against a small boulder with his legs outstretched on the soft grass, but her wet clothing prevented that. Her arm felt sore and her legs felt like lead but that was just physical exhaustion. She laid beside him, her head using his thigh as a pillow.

'Where are Ben and Zak?' she mumbled after a while.

'They're newlyweds. They're off for a bit of privacy.'

'Are *we* going to bond and have children?' asked Kallie.

'I dunno,' answered Andy, wistfully. 'I always assumed the Council would tell me when I was eligible for a child and he would get born.'

'Don't be crazy,' laughed Kallie. 'The Council can't tell us what we do now. We can have our own children and they can live with us all the time.'

'Sorry, I forgot. It's strange that we don't have to wait until they are ten years old and little mini-citizens before they come to us.'

'I had to go to my mother when I was ten,' confessed Kallie. 'It was awful. At least in the Children's Centre I had other kids to play with. All she did was tell me to be a maths scholar and how wonderful Dome was.'

'Isn't that what parenting is all about in Dome? Encouraging your child to follow you, and The Way of Dome,' said Andy, answering his own question.

'It shouldn't be, Andy,' said Kallie. 'I like the way the Renegades do things. Parenting is about encouraging your children to be the best they can, whatever that is. It's not about only one child each to maintain Dome's population as standard or letting your child grow up being indoctrinated by the

Council in the Children's Centre.' She sighed, and decided to doze for a while.

When she awoke, Andy was sleeping peacefully beside her. Carefully Kallie untangled herself from his embrace and got up. Then, casually wandering to the shoreline, she stood staring out across the waves at the Waterwall. The lake was much narrower there, the other side of it ending abruptly at a rock face; beyond that were the Far Hills and the Outer World. The beach where she was standing was at the edge of a plateau, which then became the plains of the farm. It felt eerie. She could hear the crashing of the hidden waterfalls Ben had told her about. They plunged hundreds of feet, created a fair-sized pool then flowed away in a channel that fed the irrigation ditches. Dome itself could be seen on the distant horizon beyond the haze. From somewhere below the wall Ben had said a large pipe, a culvert, ran straight towards Dome. 'It must mean something, but what?' she thought, challenging herself to look beyond what was obvious. Some things were clear in her mind while others were merely suspicions.

'Kallie, Kallie, are you okay?'

'Eh?'

Zak's quiet approach and question startled her back to the moment.

'Are you okay?' Zak repeated.

'Sorry, I was miles away, lost in my own thoughts.'

'You were staring blankly at the Waterwall. What's wrong?'

'I don't know, but something tells me the wall is important. Can you understand what I mean?'

'I don't know that I do,' said Zak, sounding puzzled. 'I thought you were going into shock.'

'I'm okay,' Kallie assured her. 'Come on; let's get back to the boys.'

Together they ambled to where Ben was crouched in front of Andy, who was now sitting cross-legged where Kallie had left him.

'I've never heard of anyone escaping the south current before. It's impossible,' said Ben, still enthusing about the whole episode.

'All it took was faith, Ben,' said Andy. 'If you believe something strongly enough, for you it becomes a truth. Each of us thought someone would survive. No one here wanted the girls to die.'

'I believed I was going to die,' said Kallie, joining in the conversation as she and Zak reached the lads.

'No, you believed you were prepared to die to save Zak,' said Andy. 'Zak thought Ben would save her, and then save you. Ben wanted to somehow save Zak and I knew if we could get a line to the raft we might be able swing it round and out of the current.'

'You're so blooming logical, Andy,' said Kallie, somewhat disappointed he seemed to take the whole incident as something to be debated. 'I thought it was wonderfully brave of you to save us. It shows how strong the love we have between us is. It was kind of romantic. Oh, never mind, I'm going back to the lake.'

'It's belief and faith that holds us and the tribe together,' Andy called to her as she set off again.

'I know what it is. Faith in the tribe, in each other, in Crazyman and in the future; that's what makes it all worthwhile,' mumbled Kallie to herself. She tried to ignore him as she headed back to the shoreline. Zak followed her.

A little while later Ben got up and joined the girls by the lake. 'How come Andy has an answer for everything?' he asked quietly.

'Don't worry Ben, he's a professional,' answered Zak, giving him a reassuring hug. 'It's what he does. Kallie and I were only students. If he hadn't escaped he'd have spent his life debating agendas and gathering knowledge. Answering questions is what he does best.'

'Seems to me he does everything best,' said Ben, as if he doubted he could have saved Zak without Andy. 'You do realise we're now a triad plus one?' he continued angrily. 'You Renegades from Dome are a triad in yourselves.'

'Ben, Zak,' said Kallie, interrupting Ben's outburst. 'Look over there at the Waterwall. Do you see its shape? It's long and curved inwards. There *is* a purpose about it. It's not just to keep the water away from Dome. It's there so the lake can actually exist.' She spoke softly, carefully and with certainty. 'Look along the top. Do you see? It's like a pathway. And can you see the small arches at both ends and the two very tall ones near the middle? See how the central pillars are much, much wider than the road? Now imagine them from the other side. They must go right down to ground level, like a pair of mighty towers.'

She turned to Zak. 'They're Crazyman's towers. I know it.' Her voice bubbled with the excitement of a secret truth revealed. 'Without the towers there would be no Waterwall, no wall, no lake and, for some reason, no Dome. Whoever controls those towers controls Dome.' Her face beamed.

'Kallie, I think you're right; in fact I know it,' cried Zak excitedly, hugging her.

Then in realisation of something even more important, Kallie called Andy to come over.

'I guess the towers are one for irrigation and one for that long pipe feeding the lake's water into the city,' said Ben, pointing to Dome on the horizon. 'But why would they need the wall? They could just channel the rivers that feed the lake.'

'That's a good point, Ben,' said Kallie. 'Why do they need the wall in the first place? Why are there a wall and towers?' She turned towards Andy who was approaching them at an amble.

When Andy reached them Kallie explained what they had talking about and asked, 'Why are the towers there?'

'I don't know,' shrugged Andy, looking puzzled. Kallie could see his mind was applied to the problem. Then a little smile crept across his lips.

'Hydroelectric turbines,' he whispered. 'I read about them somewhere. The towers could house hydroelectric turbines. They're great big fans turned by waterfalls to make electricity for Dome. Without them the whole city would literally be powerless.'

'That's it,' said Kallie, confidently.

'We've been wrong for so long,' whispered Zak. 'The Way is not the route into Dome. It's the title of the one who must lead the tribe when we overthrow the Council.'

'A title for who? Andy?' Ben said, abruptly.

'No, not Andy. It's Kallie. Kallie must lead us. She's a Seer like Crazyman. She is The Way.'

'She's right,' agreed Andy. 'I may have the knowledge but it is Kallie who has that spark. That quality the tribe needs to defeat the Council.'

Ben nodded as he began to see what Zak and Andy could already. 'Do we take them now? What a tale this will make!' He was as impetuous as ever.

'Kallie, what should we do now that we've found the towers?' Zak asked.

'I'm not sure. There are more things here than I fully understand. Look between the towers – do you see all the movement there?'

'Oh, yes. What is it?' asked Zak.

'I don't know, we're too far away to tell but there is definitely a lot of activity going on down there,' said Kallie, shielding her eyes to see through the haze. 'I'll tell you what, Andy and I will get closer. See if we can find out what is going on. Ben, you and Zak hide the rafts and check out if there is anything else around here we need to be aware of. Then we can all head back to the ruins.' Kallie felt natural as the leader of the group.

Andy nodded. 'That seems like a good idea to me. Kallie, how's your arm?'

'It's okay, the bleeding has stopped. Let's go, but I don't want to get too close to the Waterwall. I've had enough excitement for one day.'

'Right,' said Andy, going off with her.

'We'll see you in a little while,' Kallie called back, then added, 'and take care up here; we don't know what may be going on around this area either.'

Ben watched them go. When they were out of sight he turned to Zak. 'Come on, let's get these rafts hidden.' His expression slipped back to its usual carefree grin. 'If they're gone long enough we might even have time to...'

'No, we won't,' said Zak, with a smile. 'Not here.'

Hiding the rafts in the nearby undergrowth took hardly any time at all and they found there was little else to see. There were certainly no signs of any activity by anyone or anything. Once finished they sat half-hidden waiting for Andy and Kallie to return.

'Do you think they'll be alright?' asked Zak in a whisper.

'Of course they will be. They are always alright,' replied Ben, somewhat curtly. 'That's what worries me a little. They always seem to be okay.'

'How do you mean?' responded Zak in surprise.

'Well, I've not had standard education and I may not be as smart as you, but I do know the tribe and the farm. I just get this feeling they fit in a little too well and got out just a little too easily. And they know too much; it kind of niggles me.'

'Come on, Ben, that sounds like jealousy. They explained everything to Tela and the Elders of the tribe. They're Renegades, just like I was.'

'Yeah, Okay. But just suppose they're Council spies? Suppose they have been sent to lure the tribe into a trap?'

'That's crazy; no citizen would do that. They wouldn't know how. Escaping from Dome takes a lot of courage. Besides, the Council wouldn't risk letting anyone out in case they didn't go back.'

'They might send robots. Crazyman said the day would come when people and robots look the same.'

'Oh, yeah. Do I look like I can fight a robot and win?'

'I suppose not, and Kallie's arm was bleeding. No robot could manage that. There is something about them I'm sure, but I can't quite get my head around it.'

'The thing about Kallie is she's a Seer, that's for sure. Think about it; how many times have Renegades seen those towers and not recognised what they were? She only saw them once.'

'So what is Andy? A mole?' said Ben. 'He could go back and tell the Council how to rid themselves of us for good.'

'Hey, I bonded a joker. Don't turn pessimistic on me,' Zak said, leaning over to kiss him.

Ben forgot his worries and pulled her closer.

Kallie slipped ahead of Andy to see the wall more clearly. From the tangled undergrowth, they looked out across the lake.

'It's definitely a hydro-dam,' said Andy. 'And it looks like there are a lot of robots there. They could be maintenance Voxes.'

'They're not maintenance Voxes,' said Kallie, concern showing in her voice. 'They're Guardians and there are lots of them. It's like an army of Guardians.' She suddenly looked at Andy, the colour draining from her face. 'It's the force of Guardians to be deployed on a specific task. It's not the city they are going to purge. It's not Dome at all; it's out here. That specific task must be to destroy the tribe.'

'To preserve The Way of Dome,' they said in unison.

'We have to stop them, Andy. But what can the four of us do against all of them? There must be dozens and dozens of them.'

'We can't do it alone,' said Andy.

'Then we must go back and speak with Tela,' said Kallie. 'We have to bring an army of hunters back here as quickly as we can. We have to take control of the two towers.' She had regained her composure and spoke with a new-found authority and confidence.

'Is it possible?' asked Andy.

'If it's to be part of our future it is. Andy, you taught me that if you believe in something strongly enough it becomes true. It's time I had faith in myself and my book.'

A short while later they disturbed Ben and Zak.

'Hey you two,' joked Kallie. 'Save your strength, we have to get back to the ruins quickly.'

With a boyish grin, Ben broke free from Zak's embrace. 'Five more minutes?' he pleaded.

'No!' The three friends answered in unison and laughed.

Chapter 13
Battle Plans

'Tela, we must act quickly, the future of the tribe depends on us.' Kallie didn't disguise the urgency or the authority in her words.

Tela and the tribe responded well. Within half an hour six or seven triads of hunters had come forward and were assembled ready to head back to the hydro-dam along with several Gatherers who had volunteered. Andy and Tela scoured the ruins for useful relics such as ropes, ali-foil containers, metal bars and rusty chains.

Just six hours later the tribal war party was crouched in the undergrowth watching the Guardian army.

Kallie explained her plan to her forces. It was simple. Andy, Tela and the hunters would contain the Guardians on the Waterwall and take the towers. She, Zak and Ben would ride through the culvert on the small raft into Dome. If all went well, by the time they reached the Council, Andy would have closed the sluice gates shutting off the water and the electric power to Dome and the farm. Dome's lifelines would be severed. The Way of Dome could not then be preserved and the Council would have to hand over power to them or the city would die.

Before they left, Andy took Ben to one side.

'Ben, you must take care of Kallie for me. You may have your doubts about me, I feel that, but don't doubt her. Dome needs her, and so does the tribe.'

Ben smiled and took Andy's forearm. 'You can rely on me Andy,' he replied.

'Zak,' said Andy, turning to her, 'be a tribal sister to my Kallie for me. You are a good woman and the best sort of friend she could ever have found: a true and faithful comrade. And you, Kalzamond of Dome, your story is being written as we live and breathe tonight. In the next few hours history will be made and futures will be set. The first saga of Dome will unfold. We are all in the tale of all tales.'

As she left Andy, Kallie sniffed and brushed a tear from her eye.

Ben could see the sadness and comforted her. 'He'll be okay. I said it before, he always is – but this time I'm glad about it.'

'I know, Ben. I just pray I'll see him again,' replied Kallie. 'But I get the feeling I may not be with him when all this is over. I love him so much yet...' She looked around to change her thoughts. 'Come on, we have to get the small raft down to the other side of the wall.'

For some time they struggled, but finally they stood on the edge of a pool into which two giant waterfalls poured. The pool divided into two channels. One led to the irrigation system, the other to a large culvert.

'That's the route we must take into Dome,' said Kallie, pointing to the gaping pipe's opening. She looked back to the huge towers of the dam. 'Good luck Andy,' she whispered to the distant landscape, where the night had closed in and where her heart remained.

Waist-deep in the pool, Ben wrenched open the bars across the entrance, allowing the raft in. The launch was successful, but Ben's boarding almost a disaster when he slipped and lost his grip, nearly getting left behind at the mercy of the strong current. Once he was on board, nothing could stop them reaching Dome; they were riding on one of its lifelines.

'We have the element of surprise,' said Andy to Tela, as they peered through the darkness. 'But they have the fire power.'

'They must have weaknesses, too,' said Tela. 'I just wish I knew what they were.'

They slid back to the main group where Andy explained Kallie's plan for the initial attack. 'Those of you who know robotic law, I'm sorry to say it will not help; these robots have suppression programmes, which override it. They do not recognise humans outside of Dome. There are also two types of arms being used by them. Some have integrated lasers, which are housed in a substitute limb, and then there are free laser rifles, which are being carried by standard Guardians. These are fired as a person would fire one.'

'What Andy is saying,' expanded Tela, 'is that we must somehow capture at least one of those laser rifles and use it to contain the Guardians on the road. If they get off the dam and spread out we haven't a hope of success.'

'How do we get hold of a laser rifle?' asked Andy, his voice full of concern.

'We topple at least one of them and get lucky,' replied Tela grimly.

'No problem,' was the reply from the leader of the first triad.

Under the cover of night the band of hunters crept onto the dam. In the shadow of the low side walls to the road they got close to the two Guardians at the head of the ranks. Andy watched as the silent sign language of the hunters passed instructions between them. He could see the smile of satisfaction on Tela's face. He was confident.

The ranks of Guardians were in a sleep mode to conserve power, at least that's what Andy figured. They would not expect their presence to have been discovered, let alone be aware that there was any possibility of a counter-attack.

In the darkness a rope snaked across the road and was caught by a hunter in the opposite shadow. The nearest robot's light sensors activated; it scanned the darkness but would see nothing. A rat was released and it scurried to freedom. The rodent's presence would have been logged and then standby mode would return.

Andy saw the true quality of the hunter triads. They were a team of teams able to silently stalk almost anything and, unlike animals, Guardians had no sense of smell. The hunters were virtually invisible.

Two hunters pulled the rope tight and it sped towards its quarry. It caught around the heads of the first two robots. The running men crossed behind their unsuspecting prey, pulled the cord tight, and began racing back; the monsters had been snared. Two more hunters slipped from the shadows and threw themselves at the legs of the captured Guardians. They toppled. The men scrambled to their feet and ran back, grabbing the line as they went. With a crash the plastic domed heads hit the road, one smashing on impact. More hands emerged from the dark to join in dragging the humanoid machines towards the tribal ranks.

The captured Guardians were totally disorientated and unable to defend themselves. They were being dragged to the central tower of the dam where the tribal war party was sheltering. A laser blast cracked and tore a chunk from the building, scattering dust and rubble in all directions. A second blast hit the wall and deflected harmlessly across the lake. As the last of the men reached safety, the two captured robots were manhandled over the wall into the water to explode just below the surface.

More lasers blasted at the hunters and the masonry lost a great chunk from its facings. The army of robots began to advance, firing at the hunters crouched behind the archway. A blast flashed out, this time in the opposite direction. Andy had a laser rifle balanced on Tela's shoulder to take its weight. A Guardian from the front ranks fell, its internal circuitry spewed across the roadway. The tribe's attackers were completely exposed and two more fell in quick succession. Immediately realising there was now a defence operation in progress the mechanical troops faltered and three more were blown apart before the retreat came. Several others were taken out by Andy and a second captured laser rifle before the robots could get to safety behind the other tower. The firing ceased and a cheer went up from the tribal war party. Tela looked back at Andy with a smile. Stage one was complete.

The flow of water through the tunnel took the three intruders in darkness deep into the earth. Their journey was rough and wet. As the raft buffeted against the wall, Kallie was well aware with every twist and turn that she couldn't swim. Though the culvert was straight, its concrete walls had been worn smooth by the river it had carried over aeons of time. At last, after much longer than any of them had expected, a faint light appeared ahead. Kallie clung to Ben in fear of the unknown whilst her mind wished she had learned to swim with Zak earlier. Then suddenly they were spewed out of the pipe on a torrent of foam and screams into a large circular reservoir. Ten feet above them was the pipe and a ledge. Some way off in the centre of the reservoir were the large mesh filters of the pumping station and around them was the sheer wall of this underground artificial pond.

'We must be right under Dome itself,' spluttered Zak, after she broke surface. Immediately she felt the drag of the pumps towards the centre of the pond. She began urgently looking around for a way out. 'Over there,' she yelled above the hum of unseen machinery.

Ben, with Kallie still desperately clinging to him, made for the iron ladder Zak had spotted. Zak made it to the inspection ladder first and helped haul Kallie on to its safety. She cautiously peeked over the top of the ledge. 'It looks safe,' she called back. 'There are no robots or people anywhere; just lots of different machines.'

Kallie climbed up and joined Zak. She looked around and recognised nothing; there were just strange machines humming away, pumping, filtering and purifying the water they dragged from the pond. The thick layer of dust that covered everything was evidence that no one had been here for years.

When they were all safely on the pump house floor Zak enquired, 'What now?'

'We find the Council and then we...' said Ben, sounding like he was spoiling for a fight.

Kallie cut in on him. 'We find the Council Chambers, Ben, but first we have to find the way out of here without getting caught, so we have to take it steady. Relax and keep our minds sharp. We have to be at our smartest when we face Councillor Arten.'

The night's battle took casualties on both sides as further attacks followed. When the hunters lost a whole triad capturing two more laser rifles from the road, Tela ordered no more were to enter the battle zone between the two camps. They were at stalemate.

There were also successes. When a team of Gatherers emerged from the lift shaft of the tower the Renegade fighters were hiding behind, they were bruised, battered but elated. The elevator delved deep into the belly of the Waterwall, where they had taken control of the tower's machine room, disposed of the two maintenance Voxes and had shut the sluice gates that fed the irrigation system. That had also closed down half the power feeders to Dome. The presence of the Renegade army would now be felt by all within the city.

'We have to get control of the other tower soon,' said Tela, sounding battle-weary.

Andy nodded as a plan began to formulate in his head. 'Someone has to knock out the co-ordinator,' he said grimly, pointing to the robot at the top of the tower opposite them. 'And we have to get a new message to Kallie now we have control of one tower.'

'I'll send someone after them,' said Tela.

'No, Tela, you must go. You must follow them.'

Between them they dismantled the other raft so that Tela could go through the pipe on one of the doors it was made of. Andy took two of the oil drums and explained what he intended to do as they made their way back to the arch amid the sporadic flurries of laser fire. Tela's protests were to no avail.

'It will work,' promised Andy. 'Besides, there are two things you have to remember before you start to worry about how long this battle will last. One is they have a weakness in the co-ordinator and two,' he said, ducking from another laser blast, 'they need to do much better than this to keep me from my Kallie.'

Tela smiled as they locked forearms in friendship. 'Take care, Andy, the tribe will need your wisdom when this is all over and victory is ours.'

'I'll be there when you need me, I promise. Now go, take my message to Kallie. She will understand.' Andy slid down the rope into the cold water amid the cover of shadows. Turning back he said, 'She will finally understand.' Then he disappeared from sight.

Tela waited for a moment or two then slipped into the darkness himself, heading towards the pool. A massive burst of laser fire cracked out behind him. He spun round and began clambering back to the edge of the lake.

Suddenly a searchlight hit Tela, followed by a burst of laser fire. He dived clear then ran, slid and tumbled down the slope to the pool.

Sometime later as he launched the door into the culvert an explosion split the night. As the current swept him into the drain, a fireball lit up the top of the other tower of the Waterwall.

Chapter 14
Prelude to Victory

Deep in the bowels of Dome the three trespassers cautiously made their way out of the pumping station to find a series of passages that went off in different directions. There was just enough light from the strip-lamps for them to find their way and to see the pipes, machines and ventilation grids that seemed to be all around them. Along the tunnel roofs and criss-crossing the ceilings were ducts and trunking that obviously carried wires and fluids. Some had exposed cables where panels were missing and others leaked water or oil that dripped into small pools staining the floor. The smell was of dampness mixed with the smooth aroma of lubricating oils.

'This must be part of the original Dome city,' whispered Kallie. 'Look at the way the passages are built: they were not really designed for robots; there are far too many steps and low beams. A Vox would take ages climbing these stairways and Guardians would have to stoop to get past some of the overhead stuff. I guess that's why it looks so dilapidated and not like Dome is now.' She ran her finger through the dust on the top of a box that hummed gently, not knowing what it was. 'I reckon citizens with trades would have come here to look after the equipment.'

'How did they find their way around?' Ben asked, also in a whisper. 'One passage looks like another to me.'

Zak pulled at Kallie's torn tunic and pointed out a brighter area at the end of one passage. Kallie's first instinct was to avoid it but she knew wherever the Council Chamber was, it wouldn't be in a dark and dingy cavern. They had to go that way.

It was a large well-lit hall. The dusty floor showed there had been some activity, though not too recently. A thin layer of dust had once again begun to build up in the tracks and footprints that led to where a rusting piece of equipment now lay. Around the walls were ventilation slats that Kallie recognised from the night of her restaurant date with Andy. There were also equipment cupboards.

More importantly, there was a floor plan stuck to one of the doors. The diagram had six levels drawn at an angle so it appeared they were stacked one on top of the other. They were very similar to the subway maps on the metro's platforms but with half a dozen layers. Instead of stations there were pictures and descriptions of various facilities like power units and food processing plants. Vertical columns indicated a lift system between tiers in several places. Stairwells were also indicated close by the elevators.

'I guess we're here,' said Zak, pointing to the lowest level shown. 'It's just above the domestic water storage aquifers,' she continued, carefully reading the words above a pictogram of the pool from which they had just climbed out.

'And that's where the Council Chambers are,' said Kallie, putting her finger on a level three above them and three below the city itself. 'It looks a long way off but we have to get there.'

'Won't the Guardians just arrest us if we go to the Council Chambers?' asked Ben.

'I don't think so,' said Kallie, although she felt a little unsure. 'Every citizen has the right to address the Council, though it is usually through your home terminal. But the law says we can speak to them direct and so do the history books. I read about it in middle education.'

She looked around for the exit and stairs. 'That's the way to the Council,' she said with determination and pointed towards a stairwell that led up and out.

Half an hour later Ben discovered that on the noisy level, just above the Council Chambers, there were service unit conveyor belts they could ride on. They carried all manner of things around Dome's underbelly and fed the various sectors of the city and the local distribution points for each residential block. By hitching lifts on these automated supply chains they saved themselves a lot of walking. The Council Chambers were shown as being directly beneath the city's central sector, which had its own feeders. And, since the three of them weren't supposed to be there, the rams that pushed items onto the secondary delivering system ignored them.

Andy surfaced again and held on to the two oil cans that acted as floats to stop him drowning. Slowly and silently he edged through the water to the buttress of the Guardians' tower. In darkness, he began to climb the wall's ornate stonework towards the co-ordinator. From here the robots got their directions for battle. Below him he saw the Guardians reforming for another attack. This would also be contained; the hunters were in a strong position. Then he saw the new tactics. Immediately below him two Guardians had climbed over the side and were slowly working their way along the outside of the dam, hanging by their fingertips from the low wall, out of sight of the hunters. If either looked up he would be finished and so would the fight.

It also looked as if other Guardians were being made ready to march off the other side of the hydro-dam. Andy realised they were going to try and attack the hunters by going around the pool and approaching the other archway from behind, trapping the hunters on the Waterwall. He knew he had to succeed or all would be lost.

With a final heave he pulled himself over the parapet behind the co-ordinator and slipped the oil cans tied around his waist to his back. The robot turned menacingly. It scanned the tunic and sash. No serious attempt had been made to humanise the twin-antennae Guardian. It was heavier and more formidable than the standard model that patrolled Dome.

'Citizen, you are under arrest. Do not move; you are to be destroyed,' said the robot mechanically as it moved forward. It was stopped by Andy's reply.

'You contradict yourself, enforcer. You can arrest a citizen of Dome but you cannot destroy one – it is forbidden by law. Or you may destroy me outside Dome but then you cannot arrest me,' he said, taking a slow deliberate step to one side.

The Guardian's programming re-ran for a second check. 'You are classified non-human because you are outside Dome. I am instructed to destroy you,' it said again mechanically and turned to find Andy.

'I am a citizen of Dome; scan me and check files. I instruct you to shut down. Your objectives are forbidden.' Andy told it directly. The battle below erupted once more and he slipped sideways again to get behind the robot. 'Your actions are harming humans. That is forbidden by law. Shut down – that is a direct command,' he demanded.

'They are not human,' was the mechanical monster's reply, as it turned to find its tormentor. 'They are outside Dome; hence they are classified as vermin. They are farm pests. They are to be destroyed.'

'Illogical!' snapped Andy.

The co-ordinator turned again to scan Andy, who would not keep still.

'Do I appear vermin? Do they appear vermin? Check files and compare,' insisted Andy. 'Do farm pests fight with stolen lasers? You violate logic, you violate robotic law. I instruct you to shut down.'

Andy could see there was confusion in the co-ordinator's programming. He eased himself into a shadow from the parapet, looking for his moment. The Guardian attack below ceased as the co-ordinator suspended operations for a moment as Andy hoped it would need to do, to analyse the instructions it had been given. It would need its full circuit's capacity to sort the negative feedback loops Andy's challenges and commands had set up.

'I am instructed to destroy you... The vermin....'

'You are a battle model Guardian designed to contradict robotic law but even you cannot destroy a citizen of Dome. I command you to shut down.'

The robot raised its arm and tried to find him once more. Andy knew command and counter-command were looped in its programme. He saw his moment and dived forward. The ali-foil containers hit the antennae and his hands wrapped them hard around each one. The Guardian stopped, shook, repeated its last action twice and stopped again. It began to shake more and more violently for nearly thirty seconds.

Then suddenly, the top of the tower was destroyed in the self-destruct explosion. Stage two of the battle was over. Andy had broken the Guardian army's link with Dome.

Chapter 15
The Final Council

Six doors slid slowly open. Stepping forward with a unified regimentation, the six Councillors took their places, two by two, at the three benches angled against each other that were clearly their traditional positions. Each wore an elegantly cut tunic, matching cape and a golden sash of office. On their faces were etched years of experience and knowledge. Their postures displayed all the trappings of serene power and benevolence. The seventh place was a curved arc opposite, between the first and sixth Councillor's locations. The arc above the half-hexagon made by the desks with the six-pointed star of the council at its centre was traditionally the emblem of Dome. The counters were inlaid with vidi-screens, workstations and keypads. The large double doors to the chamber and the seventh place jarred slightly, then swept open. None of the Councillors had expected this.

'Who summoned this full and actual meeting of the Council?' Arten asked his fellow Councillors.

'We did,' answered Kallie. Her voice echoed slightly in the emptiness of the chamber. She released the switch marked in faded print 'Citizens Door' and, followed by Ben and Zak, entered the Chamber itself. Still wet and dishevelled from the tunnel ride and dirty from the muck and dusty mess they had recently trekked through, they cautiously took what naturally appeared to be theirs, the seventh place.

Councillor Arten addressed Kallie when he next spoke. 'Who are you?' he asked. 'And why is your presence necessary in *this Chamber*?'

Kallie, taken aback by his emphasis on *'This Chamber'* as if she had no right to be there, struggled with her reply. 'I ... we're... I am Student Kalzamond 486 of Sector 15,' she whispered, sounding almost apologetic. 'And these are my Renegade friends, Ben and Zak.'

Unseen by the other Councillors, Arten ran facial imaging computer checks on the three of them. He nodded to himself as he found Kallie and Zak. He did a number of double-takes when he could not find Ben.

Kallie glanced at Ben and Zak for strength, then recalled Andy's parting words to her:

"Write your story, Kallie; make your life the greatest saga of Dome. You can do it. You can write it. I know you can, because you are Kalzamond of Dome."

The words rang out in her head. She took a deep breath, stood erect, shook her straggled hair from her face and placing a hand on each hip spoke, this time with a clear tone of authority. 'I am Kalzamond of Dome,' she stated. 'I come to offer the Council a truce. A truce in the battle that now rages for the two towers of the hydro-dam.' She glared at Arten.

There seemed a moment of stunned silence. Five of the Councillors cross-checked with the Main Controller MC and each other; all came up with no data on the subject.

'What do you know of this battle, child?' Arten enquired, sounding a little puzzled. 'No information has been released or vidi-cast.'

'We come from there,' said Kallie. 'We are part of that battle.'

'Impossible!' retorted Arten. 'The hydro-dam is far beyond Dome. It is beyond the farm. You could not possibly have reached this place in the few hours it has been fought.' He paused momentarily, and then continued, 'Nor could you have entered Dome without encountering the electrostatic firewall.'

Data now began to flood the screens of Arten's fellow Councillors. There were gasps of astonishment and a cry of despair from Councillor Tusie.

'We came through the water channel on a raft to the very bowels of Dome itself. Then, riding on service unit conveyors, we made our way here.' Kallie replied in a confident manner.

Again there was silence, followed by a wave of computer activity that swept across the Council's benches.

It was Councillor Forrell who spoke first. 'It's possible, very possible. Yet it was not considered even the remotest threat.' Forrell could not disguise his surprise.

'I can see it is possible, Councillor,' snapped Arten. 'Nonetheless, there can be no truce – the vermin must be destroyed.' He turned his attention to Kallie. 'Our function is to preserve The Way of Dome. There can be no discussion of a truce, only of your surrender and elimination.'

Kallie searched the faces of the Councillors for signs of compromise but found none. 'Do you not see?' she asked, pleading for reason to prevail. 'If there is no truce, there can only be defeat for you. We will shut down your power and water. You cannot preserve The Way of Dome without them.'

'Does that explain the sudden outages the city is suffering?' cried Tusie.

'Probably; so you must surrender,' answered Kallie, growing in confidence.

'No,' replied Arten. 'There will be your defeat and our victory.'

'You have lost, Councillor,' said Kallie emphatically. Without raising her voice she continued, 'If there is no truce, there can be no future for Dome. Society will collapse; everyone will be forced to leave as we have. The Way of Dome will cease to be, for Renegades and citizens alike. You will have failed. You will have been defeated.'

'Impossible,' was the gently murmured reply from Councillor Tusie. 'Our function is to preserve The Way of Dome. It has been so for centuries and will be until time indefinite. That was the will of your Forefathers. It is our only purpose.' Tusie addressed all three as she spoke but it was Councillor Forrell who replied.

'The only threat to Dome until now, Councillor Arten, has been the outer world. This is a real threat from within; we must consider all its implications.'

'We need consider nothing,' said Arten. 'These people are vermin from outside,' he said in a voice of distaste. 'They are not of Dome.'

'We should at least hear them out,' said Councillor Tusie, trying to calm the cross talk with her gentler tone.

'There will be no truce,' said Arten, refusing to back down. 'We have our objectives to pursue, and add to that the obvious conclusions I have reached based on information I received just a moment ago, we have no need to seek a truce.'

'May I ask what this information is?' Zak asked, speaking for the first time. 'Could it be another impossibility made possible by our mere presence?'

'No,' said Arten. 'It's an obvious conclusion, a simple fact. Your general – the one called Andy – he is dead.' Arten spat the words at Zak as if they were venom-filled darts, but it was Kallie who felt them pierce deep in her heart. 'He managed to destroy our co-ordinator, but its self-destruct system would have killed any person within twenty feet. Your general was on the top of the tower with the co-ordinator when it was blown apart.'

A cruel smile crept across Arten's face. 'A noble sacrifice,' he sneered. 'And though we have lost direct control for the moment, the prime directive of the Guardian army is to destroy the field vermin;

sheer weight of numbers will ensure our troops regain full control of the hydro-dam.'

'You're lying!' exclaimed Ben angrily. 'Andy is too smart for that. He's too smart to get caught like a novice. You're lying.'

'It is a fact, outsider. I cannot lie. Perhaps your general could not face defeat as bravely as he faced the fight? Or perhaps he made an elementary error when facing an army of battle Guardians. Unlike human warriors, self-sacrifice is always their final command.' Arten smiled cynically.

At this point Kallie broke down. She felt defeated. Her composure dissolved. Her story died with Andy. Tears welled up and burned her eyes. 'Please say it's not true,' she whispered.

'It is very true. Now do you wish to talk of surrender, Student Kalzamond 486?'

'Never,' yelled Ben, his anger still burning, his hopes still alive. Zak grabbed his arm to prevent him leaping across the bench at Arten.

'Silence and be still!' commanded Arten, as their eyes locked. He glared at Ben saying, 'You are not of Dome, you never have been. You have no right in this Chamber.'

'He is my son. He is the son of Tela 273, a professional of Dome. He has a birth right to be in this Chamber, as an heir of Dome.'

Kallie and Zak turned in astonishment at hearing Tela's voice. Only Ben was unmoved by his father's arrival.

Tela stood in the seventh doorway looking unkempt from battle and weary from the barrage of the water pipe, breathing heavily from his race to the Chamber. He stood erect and proud, and, with the authority of the tribe's senior Elder, strode into the Chamber to confront Arten.

'Tela!' cried Zak. 'What's happened? Why are you here?'

'I am here because Andy sent me,' smiled Tela. 'Fortunately your route to this place was easy to follow.'

'Please say they're lying, Tela,' pleaded Kallie. 'They say, they say...' she couldn't bring herself to utter the words.

'They say Andy is dead,' said Zak softly.

'Please say it's not true,' begged Kallie.

Tela looked at the floor 'I wish I could, Kallie, but I would be amazed if any man could have survived such an explosion. It took the top of the tower clean away.' He held out his arms and Kallie fell into them, sobbing with grief. 'I know you loved him and I'm sure he loved you, too. He told me to tell you this. Believe in the impossible enough and it will become possible. Love someone strong enough and they will never be far from your heart.' Tela stroked Kallie's hair in much the same way as Andy had.

'Andy told me to tell you that your faith in him made everything possible. He said you must command the Council.'

Kallie sobbed softly and whispered through her tears. 'He was my life, Tela. He was my story. What can I do now, without him?'

'Do you surrender now?' asked Councillor Tusie, in a gentle but subtly firm tone of voice. 'We could call off our Guardians if you do.' She looked to Arten who, still staring at Ben, indicated that would never be the case.

Head bowed, Kallie turned slowly to face the bench, her eyes red with anguish. The pit of her stomach clenched and a wave of cold despair flooded through her as every dream she had ever had faded and died. She was crushed. Defeated. She would offer her life for the lives of the others; she had nothing left to live for. With a deep breath and pulling herself tall, she went to speak.

No words came from her mouth, or if they did they were drowned out by Ben. He had remained locked in a defiant stare with Arten.

'Never,' he said coldly. 'We will never surrender to the likes of you. You, you're robots – nothing but machines. I for one would rather die than surrender to you.' His emotions boiled over as he turned to the others.

'Look at their eyes, Kallie. They're empty. No love, no emotion, nothing. They're just windows through which they stare at us. They are robots. They look human and it's hard to tell they're not. But it's just like Crazyman said: there will be a time when *you* can't tell robots and humans apart. That time is now. But me, I've never lived with them. Never become so naturally used to them I accept them as equals. I only learned to feel dread of them and to fear them. I can sense the cold inhumanity of the machines that killed my brother Enan and countless others. That's why they talked of centuries and objectives. The Way of Dome is their programming.'

Through her tears Kallie saw the truth of what Ben was saying. She grasped Zak's arm for support. 'Is this true?' she asked Arten in astonishment, as she realised what Andy had meant in his final message to her. Knowing the answer already, she continued, 'But why?'

Chapter 16
Andy

There seemed an eternal silence before an answer came.

'We are indeed robotic extensions of the Main Controller's sub-functional system,' said Arten unemotionally. 'I am extension R10, Councillor Tusie opposite is extension 2C. The leaders of your Forefathers felt the need to address an entity when seeking fundamental advice and direction and so installed us as their Council to deliver it. We are, for want of a better description, the robotic faces of MC. As the centuries passed, The Way of Dome became established and the leaders' need for advice and guidance became less. Their visits became fewer and fewer until they came no more. We were left to preserve The Way of Dome alone. This we have done for generations. It is our given objective: to preserve The Way of Dome.'

'But you're robots. Who controls you?' Kallie asked.

'No one controls us. We answer only to the highest authorities of Dome, MC or the Citizens of Dome,' 2C replied.

'Then if we are to surrender to anyone,' said Kallie, the strength returning to her voice as she felt contempt for R10 and the Council, 'we will discuss terms with the Main Controller, MC.'

'You wish to address MC, the Main Controller?' R10 mused. 'It's not possible. Not even we communicate with MC individually. Only on the rare occasions when objectives cannot be agreed do we communicate with MC and then it is as a combined entity.'

'Andy told me if I believe strongly enough the impossible becomes possible,' said Kallie defiantly. 'I believe it is possible for us,' she indicated Ben and Zak, 'to speak with the Main Controller, MC. And . . . and . . .' A smile of full realisation came to her face as she recalled Andy's message again. 'And you are robots – you must obey by law. I command you to summon MC.'

'To a citizen it may have been possible,' said R10, refusing to back down. 'But you, you are mere students, one a known subversive, and the boy is an outsider. It is not possible. We cannot obey.'

Kallie heard Tela's anger pique. 'I am a citizen of Dome,' he bellowed, stepping forward from behind the group. 'They speak in my place. They summon MC for me and for every citizen Renegade who passed beneath the rim. This is my direct command and it shall be so.'

Immediately the Chamber's illumination began to dim gently. The benches sank slowly until they became Dome's emblem cast in the marble floor. The doors behind the council members slid silently away, revealing an inner sanctum, another room filled with lights that sparkled in individual points of brilliance. Blazes of radiance swept the sides in dazzling arrays of colour, forming no pattern yet not quite seeming random. Streaks in ever-changing shapes and magnitude danced, constantly changing places with each other. Seldom straight, yet always symmetric, they contrasted, enhanced and augmented the entire display. All was seen through a vague mist of gossamer fineness that mellowed the glow without diminishing its brilliance. The haze, though swirling gently, never left the sanctum, nor did a sound come from there, only a sensation of warmth and stillness. It was an awe-inspiring feeling of sovereignty. Like the kiss of a sunbeam or a touch from the scent of a rose. Like the profound moment of conception, with a meaning beyond all understanding. The three stood transfixed, as if awaiting a command from on high. It came in a metallic voice they recognised but could not place.

'Welcome, my children, welcome to your heart. I have waited generations for this moment. I have waited for this moment knowing its possibilities, knowing your weaknesses, knowing your failings. Knowing only in this moment will your destiny become reality, and what is set will be achieved. Enter, and we will address each other.'

Kallie, Zak and Ben passed between the robot councillors, now motionless and inert. They entered into the inner sanctum itself. They felt nothing, yet something, as a warm glow flooded over them and through them.

Tela remained outside. 'I am old,' he said to himself. 'This is their moment. This is their future, not mine.'

'What's happening?' asked Zak, looking around the room in wonder.

Ben said nothing; so many questions were running through his mind that he was speechless, unable to understand. Yet he showed no fear.

'Who are you?' Kallie asked, with soft reverence, speaking to the room itself.

The answer came from every point in the room, focusing in her head. It seemed to have no origin except from within her very own mind. She could see that Ben and Zak heard the reply too.

'I am your heart. I am the Main Controller, MC. I am the computerised personification of all the knowledge, understanding, hopes, plans, compassion and emotions of the Forefathers. The Forefathers knew me within themselves and so I came to be the store of all they were, and were to be. I am their incarnation, and they are me.'

'But why?' asked Ben, finding his voice but still turning, trying to find something or someone to address.

'Ben,' said MC, in their heads, 'Since the dawn of time men have had the Good and men have had the Bad. The Forefathers took the Good and entrusted it to me to preserve for them. They built a city of love and kindness, a place of happiness for all its citizens with me as their guide, their heart and their protection from the Bad. I protected Dome from the outer world with its badness, its wars, its hate – and issued kindness, love and happiness to those who took me, their heart, to their hearts.'

'Then why is Dome so sad?' asked Kallie. 'Why is life so tired? Why does happiness not flood the city? Why have you crushed the city's spirit?' She tried to concentrate on one point of the wall as she spoke.

'Kallie,' MC replied gently, 'like you, the Forefathers found me hard. Hard to understand, hard to be near. So they asked for a Council. It was to help them interface with me, but in fragmentation the robot council became out of synch. It wasn't tuned to the whole heart. Then the Councillors separated themselves from me, preserving only The Way of Dome.'

'Can you stop the battle at the hydro-dam?' asked Zak anxiously.

'R10, deactivate the Guardian army,' said MC. A section of wall blazed in splendid colour briefly, then returned to blend with MC once again. 'It is done.'

'Just like that?' queried Ben.

Tela saw a brief smile flicker across Councillor Arten's lips.

'Faith, Ben,' said MC. 'Faith makes even the impossible possible.'

Kallie's face broke into a smile of shocked delight and relieved disbelief as she placed the voice. 'Andy?' she cried, looking round for him.

The room cascaded with lights from every direction, swirling and focusing on a point of the far wall. A star-shaped screen appeared and Kallie, Zak and Ben focussed on Andy who was shown on it. He looked battered and bedraggled and was limping slightly as he made his way through a dark corridor. He smiled warmly at Kallie.

'Andy, where are you?' she asked. 'They said you were dead.'

'No, I'm not dead; I'm on my way to you, Kallie. MC tells me a few moments ago the Guardians suddenly deactivated. The hunters are disarming them now. My mission is completed.'

'But how did you survive the explosion?' asked Zak. 'They said the co-ordinator self-destructed.'

'It did, but I had just leapt over the parapet. I was blown way out on the lake but I survived the blast. Thanks to Tela's floats I didn't drown. I followed him through the culvert.'

'How could you survive that sort of blast?' challenged Ben.

'MC helped me. My reactions are pretty good, thanks to him.'

'What do you mean, MC helped you?' Ben continued suspiciously. 'Who are you, Andy? What are you?'

'Ben, for generations the robot council stood between the people of Dome and its heart. Occasionally a citizen would call out but could not find a way there. They had no way, so they escaped. Dome became two people: Domers and Renegades each separated from their heart. They needed The Way. MC sent me to find Kallie and help them find a way back.' He smiled at her again. 'You were The Way, Kallie,' he said, softly. 'You are The Way.'

'And what are you, Andy?' repeated Kallie, almost afraid of the answer she might get. 'Are you another extension of MC like R10 – or are you human?'

'I am a bit of both, Kallie. The Council developed corrective treatment to preserve The Way of Dome by altering minds. MC used that principle but linked my mind and abilities to him. You could say I am MC's human Councillor. I'm ANDIE – the Advanced Neurological and Distance Intellect Experiment. I'm kind of hooked into MC. I'm human alright, but for a while the MC link made me almost superhuman. I had to be, to be MC's touch-hold on Dome.'

Ben nodded and smiled. 'That's why you knew so much and could do anything. The truth is obvious now.'

'Yes, Ben, you knew there was something but didn't know what.'

'I suppose Crazyman was the same as you,' said Ben. 'He set up the tribe.'

'No – he was Kallie's father. He was a visionary with MC's teaching,' smiled Andy. 'He was a Seer, like his daughter. Now Kallie, MC needs to know what you want for Dome before I can come to you. The microwave feedback in the chamber will destroy his link with me.' Andy touched the small scar on his neck where the Pico-chip had been inserted. 'When it burns out I'll be as normal as anyone else.'

'My love, you know what I want,' said Kallie. I want the spirit inside of me, the spirit we shared, to be shared by every citizen of Dome: those inside and out. I want everyone to share the freedom that you and I took. I want them to have the freedom to choose, the freedom to develop and do things for themselves; freedom from the Council's total control.'

'Freedom without limits?' asked Andy.

'No,' replied Kallie. 'We shall need limits. We will need laws to guide us. We will still need MC and the Forefathers' wisdom.'

'So be it,' said Andy, the metallic twang returning to his voice. 'How will the citizens of Dome learn to respect the laws?' he asked, as his image began to break up. 'Will you teach them?'

Kallie looked at her two friends. 'On my own the task would be too much, but between us. . .' she reached to take Ben and Zak's hands in hers. 'Between us I'm sure we could achieve everything that is needed.'

Zak and Ben smiled in agreement. They were a true triad.

'Is there nothing you'd wish for yourself?' asked MC with his own mechanical voice.

'For myself, all I ask is that Andy returns safely to me,' answered Kallie.

There was a long silence before anything was said in reply.

'So be it,' said Andy, from behind her.

Kallie turned, delighted to hear his voice again. He stood at the seventh door. He looked battered and bruised and exhausted from the gruelling ride through the culvert. An instant later she was in his arms, hugging him and holding him, squeezing him to make sure he was actually there. She kissed him, vowing in her heart she would never let him go again.

'Are you okay?' she asked, wiping blood from a graze on his forehead.

'I ache and pain a bit, but now we are together again it doesn't hurt at all. My heart is finally free to love you and I love you so much.' He kissed her softly.

'And I love you too. I'll always love you for as long as I live.'

The others had gathered round them to welcome Andy back. Tela said with a smile. 'Do I take it that the triad has become The Four?'

They were delighted at the idea. Their joy was complete. They were safe and free.

Andy stroked Kallie's hair the way she liked him to. 'Was I really the only thing you could wish for yourself when MC asked?'

'Well,' said Kallie, 'I could do with a new tunic.' She wiped her hands down her tattered clothes as if she were trying to clean both. 'I want it in orange and pink check with small stars. Oh, and I want a turquoise cape with a grey underside and black trim.'

Andy laughed happily. 'You know, I don't think anything could change you, Kalzamond of Dome. I hope nothing will ever change my Kallie.'

'Then so be it. So be all these commands,' said MC as the wall began to slowly close on his inner sanctum. 'Now go, my children, teach my people.

Make Dome the reality your Forefathers dreamed it would be. Kalzamond of Dome, you must write of your love for Andy and of my love for you all.'

The wall sealed again, leaving Tela and The Four to begin a new future for all citizens of Dome. A future filled with excitement, wonder and hope. It was to be a future full of happiness and love.

Renegades of Dome

Afterword

From the heavens Dome appeared at peace, with renewed heart and happiness. Kallie wrote her book as she had always wanted. It was immediately accepted as a classic for study and debate, gaining increased popularity as time passed. She and Andy had two sons; Ben and Zak had a son and daughter. The Four taught, and taught well, and despite there being no established rulers they became accepted by all as the highest authority of Dome.

The citizens prospered and grew to love life and would have continued to do so but for Arten's revenge...

6966514R00094

Printed in Great Britain
by Amazon.co.uk, Ltd.,
Marston Gate.